also by bertice berry

I'm on My Way but Your Foot Is
on My Head: A Black Woman's
Story of Getting over Life's Hurdles

Sckraight from the Ghetto:
You Know You're Ghetto If . . .

You Still Ghetto: You Know
You're Still Ghetto If . . .

Redemption Song

Jim and Louella's Homemade
Heart-Fix Remedy

harlem moon

broadway books

new york

HARLEM MOON
BROADWAY

the haunting

of hip hop

a novel bertice berry

This is a work of fiction. The names, characters, incidents, and most places are the products of the author's imagination and are not to be construed as real. Although part of the story is set at the very real, very hip House of Tina restaurant, the actual restaurant is not in New York City. There is also no Tubman Terrace in New York City. While I am often inspired to use names and qualities of folks I like, none of the characters in the book is based on an actual person, and any resemblance to persons living or dead is entirely coincidental and unintentional.

PRINTED IN THE UNITED STATES OF AMERICA

The figure in the Harlem Moon logo is inspired by a graphic design by Aaron Douglas (1899–1979). HARLEM MOON and its logo, depicting a moon and woman, are trademarks of Broadway Books, a division of Random House, Inc.

Visit our website at www.harlemmoon.com

First Harlem Moon trade paperback edition published 2002

Designed by Dana Leigh Treglia

The Library of Congress has cataloged the hardcover edition as follows:
Berry, Bertice.
The haunting of hip hop: a novel / Bertice Berry.—1st ed.
p.   cm.
1. Sound recording executives and producers—Fiction.
2. Harlem (New York, N.Y.)—Fiction. 3. Haunted houses—Fiction.
4. Afro-Americans—Fiction. 5. Hip-hop—Fiction.   6. Drum—Fiction.
I. Title.
PS3552.E7425   H38   2001
813'.54—dc21
00-057006

ISBN 0-7679-1212-8

10   9   8   7   6   5   4   3   2   1

For Jeanine Chambers, Keith
Chandler, Diane Dickenshied,
Selena James, Janet Hill, David
Mayhew, Earl Nicholson, Melissa
Rivera, Ph.D, Victoria Sanders,
Roberta Spivak, and all other
assistants, agents, editors, and just
good folks who give of themselves
so others may shine.

the haunting

of hip hop

prologue

No man can put a chain about the ankle
of his fellow man without at least finding
the other end of it about his own neck.
—*Frederick Douglass*, Life and Times of
Frederick Douglass, *1881*

Ngozi sat behind his wife, Bani. His legs were wrapped around hers. She leaned back, and he rubbed her large belly. "She will deliver soon," his mother said. Ngozi nibbled Bani's ear and then whispered into it. "We will have joy. Don't worry." His wife had wept for most of her pregnancy. She felt that something terrible was going to happen. Ngozi tried to persuade Bani differently. On nights like this one, calm and still, Ngozi would rub her belly and speak to his unborn son. "Yo Tayembé.

Yo Tayembé, and then you say 'Ye oh Ye Ba Ba,' " he said to Bani's stomach.

Bani laughed when Ngozi first did this. "The child cannot hear you, and you know he cannot respond."

"*Yo Tayembé,* I'm calling you, son. *'Ye oh Ye Ba Ba. I hear you, Papa,'* " he said again. "How do you know he cannot hear me?" Ngozi asked.

"How do you know it's a boy?" his wife responded.

"Woman," Ngozi said playfully, "did I not tell you that you would be my wife? Did I not tell you that I would bring you happiness? Have I been wrong? I also told you that you were with child. I knew the moment it happened."

Bani laughed. "Your mother was right to give you a woman's name. You have the thoughts of a woman."

Ngozi smiled. He'd heard this many times before. Never was he offended. "*Yo Tayembé. Yo Tayembé,*" he called to the child. "Someday you'll answer me and my stubborn wife. Bani, you'll remember this moment."

Bani was soon lulled into a sweet sleep. She would not wake up and feel Ngozi's arms wrapped tightly around her as she had on past mornings. Instead she would come to know the reason why she had been crying. Her husband, her love, would be gone from her forever.

When Ngozi saw that Bani was deeply asleep, he quietly moved himself from their embrace. He had to find the piece of wood his mother told him to look for. He had to make the drum for his unborn son. But he was making it for the son he would never see.

The drum had always been important to his people, but this one would be special. It had to be. Ngozi's mother had told him everything she had seen. Her visions started on the day he was born. On that day the memory of her grandfather appeared to her. "Name him Ngozi, for he will be a blessing."

Ngozi's mother laughed and said, "The others will think me crazy. Ngozi is a name for a girl child, she who is a blessing."

"Yes," the spirit memory of her grandfather said. "He will be a blessing, but he has been chosen to give birth." And then he was gone.

His mother had many visions after this one, but the last one, the most important one, she shared with him just before he was captured. She told him how to make the drum, what materials to use, and when to use them. The drum would be the last thing he made. "You will make this drum for your son, but you will not see him play it," she said. "Your life here will be short, but your task is great. The drum will keep you connected to your people and your purpose. You must do it, son, and you must do it right."

Ngozi was searching for just the right piece of wood for the body of the drum. Just as he bent down to touch the hollowed log that almost spoke his name, he heard something behind him. Before he could turn to see what it was, Ngozi was attacked by human hands, connected to an unnatural evil. He was carried away into the thing that his mother had spoken of. Some called it slavery; he called it death. Unfortunately for Ngozi's son, and many sons to follow, the magic of his drum would not be heard. It would be several generations before that power would be felt. Once that drum was found and played, however, it would send the wrong message.

part

one

1

the birth of Freedom

And before I be a slave, I'll be
buried in my grave and go home
to my Lord and be Free.
—*Negro spiritual*

*H*arry "Freedom" Hudson saw
the old house and wondered why it had come to mean so much
to him. He'd driven by this place many times, and it always
reached out to him and called him back. Something in the
boarded up corner house wanted him there, even in the midst
of all the gentrification and the onslaught of yuppies. It was
white flight in reverse. The park across from the brownstone
was filled with children, mostly white; an odd thing in Harlem.

Harlem belonged to him, to his people now. As he slowed and pulled up to the curb, he had a feeling that one day he'd own this house. What he didn't know was that this brownstone would come to own him.

Freedom, as he was known by the hip-hop world, was born Harry Hudson on the coldest October night New York had experienced in over one hundred years. "I'm not going to let the Devil steal my joy," his mother, Earlene, had said as she tried to start the engine of her old Chevy. The pain came suddenly and passed just as quickly. By the time she reached the hospital, she could feel Harry trying to make his way here. She drove up to the emergency room, blowing her horn and screaming in the Southern accent that had long been replaced by Brooklynese. The emergency room attendants who ran out to help her were shocked to see the crown of the boy's head on her seat.

"That boy always knew how to make his own way," Harry's mother would say later.

Harry never knew his father, and was raised by his mother and grandmother, who instilled in him a fierce independence. As a young boy, Harry always felt, even if it was not apparent to those around him, that he'd been born to do something major. He had no idea what that something was, but he knew he had to be ready. Thankfully, he was good at just about everything he put his hands to. Not just good; he mastered any area of study quickly, but he got tired of it quickly, too.

Harry finally found his "freedom" in music as a hip-hop producer, and it was his style, or "stylo" as he called it, that everyone wanted. Freedom was being pulled in so many directions now that he had little time to create. But he wasn't convinced that the record companies truly wanted or understood his creativity. They just wanted more of what had made them rich and him famous; the phat sound that put all of his artists on the charts and brought renewed prestige to a sinking music corporation. KMB Records paid him the crazy fees he asked for. Freedom laughed at the fact that his fees were based on whether or not he wanted a job. If he didn't really want the work, he charged a higher price. He'd gotten joy out of charging mad fees for tunes he made up on the spot and rejoiced when he charged people who didn't remember that they'd once told him he would never get work in the recording industry. When he first started out, he heard every rejection for every reason possible.

Initially, the industry people told Freedom that his sound was too repetitive, then they said his music didn't have a hook. After a while, Freedom ignored the criticism and just did what he felt. "Go with your heart," his mother had always told him. And it worked almost all of the time. Almost.

Freedom had many women in his life, but he only allowed his mother and grandmother into his heart. To say that Freedom was unlucky in love would be like saying Phyllis Hyman could sing. Both statements were true, but were grossly understated. Phyllis Hyman did more than sing. She ripped out your heart with every note and phrase. Phyllis made you feel all her sadness, and she made you feel like it was yours. But she warned you just the same. "Be Careful How You Use My Love" was the song Freedom thought of whenever he thought about the concept of love. There was a wall around his heart that was as ancient as the pain of black men. He wore that wall like a stick on a kid's shoulder, daring anyone bad enough to knock it off. Freedom loved women; he just didn't know how *to be in love* with them. He'd allowed himself to fall in love once, a very long time ago, but had no intention of making that mistake again.

Freedom was raised by women before psychologists had a chance to declare that not having a father was dysfunctional. For Freedom, it was heaven and he loved the balance provided by his mother and grandmother. Still, something was missing.

Shy, self-conscious, and an only child, Harry had very few playmates, so he filled the gap by creating his own imaginary ones. But to Harry these playmates sometimes seemed real, like long-gone relatives come back to play.

His grandmother was never bothered by these "playmates," but his mother didn't like it. "Stop talking to yourself, son, and go out and play," she'd tell him.

"Leave him alone, gal," his grandmother would argue, "he's talking to his people."

Sometimes at his mother's request, Harry would try to shut out the voices he heard—deep, lilting voices that told him stories and sang him songs. One day a voice called him to the window.

"Yo Tayembé," he heard the voice say. Harry didn't know the meaning of these words. They sounded familiar to him, but he couldn't exactly remember where he'd heard them.

"Yo Tayembé," the voice said again. Young Harry walked toward the window looking for the source of the voice, but didn't see anyone. He climbed into the window seat and threw open the window and stuck his head out. Still, he saw nothing. Quietly but suddenly a wave of sadness enveloped him, and he began to cry.

"Where is my father?" Harry said aloud. Just as he said this,

his mother entered the room. "Where is my father?" he repeated as he turned to her from the window seat.

"He's gone and he's been gone for a long time. Now come down from there," she said, trying to remain calm.

Harry wanted to do what his mother said, but became dizzy and lost his footing. His mother rushed to him and pulled him back in. "Ye oh Ye Ba Ba," he chanted before losing consciousness.

From then on Harry's mother forbade even the mention of an invisible playmate. Earlene argued for days with her mother, before she told her about the incident at the window. Harry's grandmother responded as Earlene assumed she would, by going into a mode of prayer and fasting, saying that little Harry was under spiritual attack. Finally, though his grandmother was too proud to verbalize it, she silently relented and decided to go along with her daughter. Grand would no longer indulge her grandson and his belief in his imaginary playmates.

Around this time Harry started communicating without speaking. He would play drumbeats on any surface with any object. In school he'd use his pencil and beat out rhythms on his notebook. At first, he played so softly that no one noticed. But the playing was accompanied by what appeared to be daydreaming, and it grew louder.

"Hey, Little Drummer Boy," his fifth-grade teacher yelled. The entire class laughed at the name and began to use it with a vengeance as children do. "Drummer" was slowly replaced with "Dumber," and so he was known throughout his school career as the "Dumber Boy," which put him just above the most unpopular boy who everyone called "Stinkweed."

Despite his nickname, Harry continued to play his beats,

luxuriating in the steady waves of music ever present in his head. One day he felt the rhythm in his heart swirl and dash whenever a certain little girl was around. Stacey Brown. For days he let her name move around in his brain, dancing in between beats. *Stacey*—*"ba ding ding"*—*Brown,* he would think, *was cute*—*"ra dat dat"*—*smart, and popular.* He didn't care that the main reason the other boys liked her was because she developed early.

"Hey, Harry," she whispered as she passed him one day in the hall. He usually heard his name from older adults, rarely from children, so when she spoke to him, he couldn't believe it, and couldn't respond. For weeks after Stacey first said his name, the shy Harry allowed himself to dream about what he'd overheard other boys say they were doing with girls. Harry imagined what it would feel like to kiss Stacey and touch her all over. Then he imagined doing "it."

Finally, after a great deal of mental preparation, Harry worked up the nerve to ask Stacey to the movies. He approached her at the end of their sixth-period class. "Stacey," he stammered, "would you . . . would you . . ." Harry was so taken with her he was unable to complete his sentence. Instead, he began to tap out beats on the books he'd been holding.

Stacey had liked Harry, but popular girls like to stay popular. Talking to Harry when no one was looking was one thing, but just as he began to drum, a group of her friends walked up and created within her the need to be nasty. "Spit it out Drummer Boy, or should I say Dumber Boy?" and without any concern for Harry's feelings, she ran off.

Harry stood frozen in the hall, and remained in the same spot until the school building closed. During those painful two hours, Harry made plans to take revenge on Stacey and all the other women he would ever come into contact with. "Someday, they're gonna want to be with me, and *I'll* be the one to run away."

It would take Freedom his entire life to realize that too often childhood wishes become the motivation for the misbehavior of adults.

2

∙◆∙

the Devil's wages

The cell phone in Freedom's car rang, and his thoughts faded back to the tune he'd promised someone.

"Peace," he barked into the phone.

"Somebody page me?" the familiar voice asked.

"Peace," he said, smiling. "Ava, I need you to get on something right away."

"What you trying to say, brother? Don't I always act quickly? That's the way I handle all your shit."

"Don't cuss. It ain't ladylike," Freedom said to his attorney.

"What do you need, my brother?" Ava Vercher was a Harvard-educated lawyer with a Brooklyn style. She was an excellent attorney and could have joined any of the top firms, but she chose to do her own thing instead. "Besides," she had always told the white recruiters, "my behind won't fit those little suits y'all have to wear." Instead, she wore African-inspired clothes such as the kind designed by Moshood that allowed more than ample room for her larger than average body. In downtown Manhattan she was considered overweight, but in Harlem and Brooklyn she was fine. Ava felt beautiful when she was with her own people, so that's where she stayed.

When Freedom told her about the house and his need to have it, she responded by saying, "You don't want that run-down piece of shit—I mean stuff—choir boy. Besides, that whole area is white as the North Pole. I happen to know on good authority that the only reason that place is empty is because it's haunted."

"Yeah, but I'm gonna haunt *you* if you don't get me that house." With that, Freedom hung up and drove off. He always knew when Ava was pulling his chain. Back when he first hired her, she'd told him that a white woman was suing him for child support. Most of her other clients would have gone into a rage, but Freedom just laughed and told her she'd better start working on a countersuit.

"How can you be so sure the kid's not yours?" Ava asked.

Freedom laughed and told her, " 'Cause I don't put my stuff in no stuff that don't look like the stuff I came from." They both laughed, and from that point on, Freedom was one of her favorite clients, and Ava by far his favorite female—not including family, of course.

As he remembered that encounter with Ava, Freedom thought that this haunted house business was just another one of her crazy pranks. But he didn't have time to think about it all now. He needed to get to the studio. He had work to do.

Freedom considered his real "work" the tunes he created for himself: music that no major record label would ever release because it was filled with the messages of the love he longed for and the revolution he dreamed of starting.

He got paid for creating music that was entirely different than the music he made for himself, but believed that he had to do what he had to do, and making the kind of commercially demanded music the record company wanted would give him the economic independence to do what he *really* wanted to do artistically.

"This whole business is about leverage, Grand," Freedom had said to his grandmother, and had then reluctantly allowed her to hear one of his recordings, a cut called "Buck Naked," that had become a number one hit for three months. His grandmother immediately went into a prayer.

"Lord, please save my child from hisself. He's walked into a place where he's not protected. Ain't no truth in it. Lead him back to wisdom, God. Call him by his name." When she was finished praying a prayer that was lengthy, even for her, Freedom told her that he had to do this kind of work until he was so popular that he would be able to do whatever he wanted.

"Grand," he'd said, "when you get a certain amount of money and power, people pay you what you want to balance the

scales back toward them. It's complicated, but you'll understand later."

His grandmother stared at Freedom long enough to make
him uncomfortable. "Son, you can't work for the Devil and ex-
pect to get heavenly wages." With that she left the place where
she'd been sitting, went to her room, and shut the door.

Now all the music Freedom produced went to the top of
the charts, and he was the most popular hip-hop producer in
the business. He'd won a Grammy for his category of music
four years in a row and he was in demand. So much in demand
that he was not free to produce anything *he* wanted to. He tried
to share his own creations with a record executive once, but was
shut down before he ever had the chance to play the demo.

"Yeah, yeah," the man told him. "We'll do that next time
out. I've got three new artists I need you to handle."

At that time Freedom had figured that he just needed more
leverage. Today, however, he remembered his grandmother's
comments and got her message loud and clear. Maybe he was
earning the Devil's wages after all.

As he drove over the bridge to the New Jersey studio, he
tried to imagine his life in what he knew would be his new
home in Harlem. When he couldn't conjure the image quickly,
he let his mind wander and started thinking about the woman
he'd been with the night before. She was wild and fine. The
physical pleasure was the memory he wanted to revisit, but then
the emotional thing hit him. She'd already called him five times,
and it wasn't even noon. He remembered how good it felt to
climax, only to have the pleasure disappear in a flash when
the woman started telling him that she loved him and had to
have him in her life. He'd tried to explain that it wouldn't work,

but it only made her cry. He hated to make any woman cry. It always made him think of the nights when he'd heard his mother crying about the things his father had either done or not done.

Freedom had once vowed to never be the rolling stone that his father had been, yet he'd become just that.

This woman's crying had the opposite effect than the one she desired, but he couldn't tell her that. Instead, he said they'd take things slowly and see where they'd end up, but then he stupidly made love to her again.

As she slept, dreaming of the life he knew they'd never have together, he slipped out of her house. *I'll deal with that later,* he told himself.

His one-night stands always left him unfulfilled and feeling shameful. He knew his grandmother would have hated the way he treated women.

While his mother had been the hardworking disciplinarian who kept him on track, his grandmother made sure that he was properly spoiled. Grand was the love of his life. "Aw, gowan and git dat boy whatever he wants," she'd say to his mother right in front of him. No matter how much his mother argued and swore to never back down, he knew that his grandmother would win. She always did.

Despite his closeness with his grandmother, Freedom and his mother shared an undeniably strong bond, and not just because they were mother and son. They were a whole lot alike, and he respected all that she was. With his grandmother, it was something else, something he couldn't put a finger on. Maybe it was her age or the era she was from. She had a way of always knowing what he needed and what he was feeling and would meet those needs with just the right look or an old song. Freedom would frequently fall asleep with his head in her lap, even when he was way past the age when that was culturally or socially acceptable. And he would tell her everything—except the way he dealt with women.

He was sure she knew that part of him, though. He would see the look on her face after he'd had one of his nights. It was a look of pure disappointment. On one balmy autumn evening after she'd given Freedom one of those looks, his grandmother passed away.

Freedom's mind went back to that night. He could still smell the meal she had cooked. Pork chops and baked beans.

"That stuff will kill you, Grand," Freedom had said. "Pork ain't nothin' but death. Death given to us by The Man. You know you shouldn't be—"

When Freedom's grandmother raised her hand and said "Don't change the subject on me, boy," he knew he was about to be lectured. Grand was always able to look at Freedom and see clear through him.

"You need to do better by women, boy," was all she finally said.

"I treat you and Moms real good." Freedom smiled to erase the disappointment that was coming from her but his grandmother wasn't having it.

"You keep trying to be the center of attention when real joy is all in the corners."

Unsure of what she meant, Freedom continued with his own argument. "Like I said," Freedom continued, "I try to take the best care of you, but you gotta help me. For real, Grand. You need to cool it with the pork. Swine is death."

Freedom's grandmother finally smiled at her grandson. "I been eating pork for way longer than the twenty-eight years you been on this planet. When it's my time, it's my time. I'm ready. Are you?" Grand asked him.

"Uh-oh, is it time for my 'Jesus is coming back' speech? Love you, Grand, but I gotta go." With that, he did. He often played that moment over again in his mind. Grand died that night in her sleep. The cause was not diabetes or high blood pressure; her cholesterol was perfect. It had been, just as Grand said, "Her time."

3

Ngozi's capture

. . . And the wicked carried
us away to captivity.
—*Negro spiritual*

*gozi felt others around him. Men
and women were crying in languages some of which he'd heard before,
but most he had not. His eyes were ready to see, but his heart was
not. Ngozi was wedged in between and chained to strangers who
were now linked together in a common suffering. Some were as young
as he was and others younger, but all were crying and screaming. He
would later learn that those who captured him would have no need
for elders, but in his village the elders were the center of life. "Mama,"*

he cried. "Why did you not tell me? Where am I, and why am I here?"

Ngozi took in his surroundings and became sick from the foul stench of waste and sweat that was around him. His own sickness added to the thick air.

Someone behind him yelled over the screams. "Brother Ngozi, it is I, Stabo."

Ngozi's heart leapt at the sound of the familiar voice, but he felt no joy. He cried, "My brother, how is it that you too have been captured?"

Stabo, who was a part of Ngozi's village and the husband of his sister, cried loudly. Then he told the tale of his capture. He told of being beaten and dragged by men he'd never seen. Fierce warriors whose markings were not familiar had brought him to the water house where they now were. "We are moving, my brother," Stabo said. "We are far from home, and I am told we will never go back again."

Ngozi was silent. He thought of what his mother had told him. He had been preparing himself for death, but this was not the death he was prepared for.

This death was the death of separation. A separation from his true self and from those who were like him. Now he knew the power of the drum, and he fully understood why his mother told him to make it. It was to be a voice that would connect those who had been captured. For although they were from different villages, different tribes, they were one people, and now they were experiencing a similar death.

Ngozi wept for the loss of the village, the loss of his family, and he wept because he had no way to tell his family where he was or what was happening. He would never be able to tell those he left behind about his life in this strange place.

Ngozi wept until he had no more tears.

4

Ava takes care
of business

If you don't know where you're from,
you can't know where you're going.
—*Pastor Ralph Buchanan*

W hat's up, my brother?" Ava said into the speakerphone. Her tone was businesslike and serious, but kind. She didn't much care for the real estate attorney on the other end of the receiver, but she respected his business savvy, and knew he would find out all he could about the house and maybe even get it for the right price.

"Mr. Campbell, I need your services, brother," Ava said to

Charles Campbell III, who had been Chucky, the neighborhood nerd, until he left for Princeton and came back white.

Charles smiled at his speakerphone and wished he could be as free as Ava. In truth he wished he could be with her. Instead, Charles had learned to act as if he liked more professional women, women who had perfectly combed hair, women who didn't laugh as loud as Ava, women who just weren't fun. But when he got right down to it, Charles wasn't much fun himself.

Whenever he'd run into someone from his old neighborhood, his mind would rush back to late-night games of hide-and-seek with a girl from down the street. Ava had a wide gap between her two front teeth, and whenever she smiled, which was almost always, Chucky wanted to take up residence right there in that gap. He could not have been more than eleven years old, but he'd observed his mother and her boyfriend, and thought he knew a little bit about love from watching them. Chucky had also heard the bigger boys talk about something called sex and how good it felt and figured if he could just kiss that girl with the gap, his life would be a whole lot better.

"Mr. Campbell," Ava said, interrupting his thoughts. "The house on the corner, across from the park. I need to know if it's available."

"Oh yeah, sorry," Charles said. "My secretary just came in. I'll get back to you in a moment," Charles said to the air. He had been so lost in thought that he heard none of what Ava had said past the initial request.

"Do you have an address?" he asked. Ava gave him the address and asked him to get back to her with the cost and other details as soon as possible.

"I heard that place is haunted, and that's why it's still empty," Ava said. Charles was now on the same page.

"You mean that house on Harriet Tubman Terrace just off the corner of One hundred thirty-eighth?" Charles asked.

"What do you think I've been rambling about?" Ava asked.

"I'm sure there is a reasonable explanation for all of those occurrences, most of which, by the way, are exaggerated," Charles informed her.

"Whatever." Ava sighed. "Get me some numbers. I may have a buyer, but it depends on the price."

"Really? When would you like to see it?" Charles asked.

"I'll get back to you," Ava told him. "Right now, I need that information for my client. Thanks," Ava said, and hung up.

Now it was Ava's turn to laugh. She would get the house for less than Charles would offer, and she'd get the city to pay for the renovations. But what really made her smile was the idea that she'd make Mr. Charles "Chucky" Campbell III remember where he was from.

5

time is running out

How long before you think he gets here?" the voice asked.

"Don't know, but it better be soon," the second voice answered. "Time is running out for our people."

"Seems like it's taken him forever to find this place," the first voice offered.

"Yes, but this is how it's to be. Everything in its time."

As Freedom got closer to Manhattan, his cell phone rang. The music was kicking from his car stereo, and it was loud enough for others to hear, even with the windows of his Mercedes SUV completely shut. He was listening to Kathleen Battle's "So Many Stars." Freedom enjoyed every kind of music.

"If you want to make phat sounds, you gotta listen to everything," he was known to say. "You get a note from here, a hook from there, the beat from the sound of some drunk trying to find his way home. The music is everywhere, but you have to listen for it," he once told a magazine reporter. For the most part, Freedom liked to talk about *his* music, but he never told anyone about the rhythms of his childhood or the voices he used to hear.

"Peace," Freedom barked into the cell phone. "Whoever's on the other end, please turn that shit down."

Elum N Nation didn't have the same need for variety that Freedom had and was blaring some gangsta rap.

"What's up?" Freedom asked the rap artist who he'd taken to the top of the charts.

"What's up?" Nation yelled. "What's up is that you were supposed to be here an hour ago." Elum N Nation took a toke of whatever he was smoking.

"On my way now. What's the rush?" Freedom asked.

"The rush is we need you to start the session," Elum said.

"On my way. Stay up. Peace," he said as he ended the call.

Freedom did everything in his own time. He was always late and often missed appointments. "You're only late once," he'd say. "Five minutes or five days, late is late. People who get pissed about time will find something else to be pissed about when you're on time," he reasoned. His relationship with time was unreasonably strained, and he had his own theory. "We should control time and stop letting time control us," Freedom liked to say. "Time ain't real. It's a construct." Now that he was important, few people argued with him.

It was a known fact in the music industry that Freedom required little time to do what he did. Other producers might show up early, but they often ran over the allotted time. Freedom showed up late and left early. He usually got the sound he needed from an artist in one or two takes. If later on, while mixing the tracks, he felt that he needed more, he simply created the tracks electronically. Once he'd even mixed his own vocals over those of the artist's. The music executives loved the results and wanted to keep it. When the record was released, it immediately went to number one.

As Freedom pulled up to the studio, a young assistant came out to meet him.

"Hi, I'm Tangy," she said between cracking sounds she made with her chewing gum. "Pleased to meet you, Mr. Freedom," she said. Her clothes were at least two sizes too small, and there was little left to Freedom's imagination.

He preferred to have something to think about, but he didn't discriminate. "Check you later," he said.

Tangy had already taken his car keys and was moving into the driver's seat. She'd park the car and do anything else Freedom wanted. These "assistants" were now part of his package.

"Everyone's waiting inside. Is there anything I can get you?" she yelled back to Freedom.

"Not right now," he said, smiling.

Elum N Nation's lyrics were like pure darkness, but the beat was righteous. There was something alluring about the beat that could even make church ladies want to "back that thang up," but once they heard the lyrics, they'd be brought back to their senses. Elum N Nation's music was misogynistic, violent, and not at all pro-black. The uncensored version of Elum N Nation's songs were banned on most radio stations, which only made them much more popular. When a radio station did play his music, there was so much foul language to be bleeped out, his tunes were called the Bleeper Songs.

"Hey stank 'bleep,' come sit on my 'bleep.' You a dumb 'bleep' nig-'bleep,' but I want it now. When I say it, bring it here cause this boy ain't gonna wait. I wanna bring slavery back cause you my Black 'bleep.' "

"What up, baby?" Elum asked when he saw Freedom walk into the studio. Elum was high and happy and the gold and diamonds that adorned every one of his fingers caught the reflection of the low light as he reached out to embrace his producer. A huge diamond-studded medallion hung around Elum's neck and swung down below his waist.

"Alright. You ready?" Freedom asked.

"I was born ready," Elum barked back.

Freedom sat down at the sound deck and got to work. Within eight hours, he had laid not just all the tracks but also Tangy the assistant.

Feeling done but not satisfied, Freedom drove back to the house on Tubman Terrace and sat in front of the place that he was determined to make his own and took in all the details.

The house would need to be renovated, but it had good bones. The front steps had begun to crumble. The ironwork was rusted, and some of the windows had been broken. But he could also see the fine work that had gone into the place. Four different faces had been carved into the bricks of the archway. The railing, while rusted, spiraled into a braid and then curved into the head of a snake. A small apple protruded from the snake's mouth. As Freedom sat watching the house, he thought he spotted a light inside. The light flickered suddenly, and though he watched the same second-floor window, he didn't see it again. Suddenly Freedom was hearing rhythms. He looked down and noticed that he was the source of the sound. Unconsciously, he was beating out rhythms on the dashboard of his SUV.

Freedom stopped himself and decided to head home and get some sleep.

Inside the Harlem brownstone, it was neither late nor early. Time was simply drawing nearer.

6

---

a little sleep,
a little slumber

> The difference between grown
> folks and babies is a nap.
> —*Mother Berry*

*F*reedom only slept a few hours
and was restless, mentally and physically, so he went for a run.

"Boy, you need to sleep to hear what the ancestors are telling you," his grandmother used to say.

"Now, Grand," Freedom always responded, "sleep is for lazy people and old folks, except *you*." His grandmother would shake her head and mumble something about fools and babies, and then go back to the task at hand.

Freedom thought about his grandmother now as he ran. Running was how he got his energy and his ideas, so he would usually run five, or sometimes ten, miles a day.

Today Freedom hummed the tune he'd been sampling and reminded himself to pull another album by the same artist. He loved sampling short phrases from cats like Sinatra, Frankie Vallee, and the Allman Brothers. Whites had stolen their whole doo-wop from us, he reasoned, so it was past time for a little payback. While other producers and musicians sampled black artists, Freedom took pleasure in ripping off the rip-offs. It was his version of restitution, his forty acres and a mule.

After he ran eight miles, he took a long hot shower and was set. Then Freedom waded through the clutter of his bedroom. His mother used to come over and "organize" his things only to be told they were already organized.

But Freedom's crib, as he called it, was in total disarray. Albums and CDs were everywhere. Videotapes and video games were piled on the floor around the cart that was supposed to house them. Clothes were strewn everywhere and so was money. It was as if Freedom had no respect for the things he'd worked hard to get. Checks, cash, and coins of all denominations lay on his bed and dresser, as if he never intended to use them. The only items that seemed to be revered were his production equipment and the photos of his mother and grandmother. The latter hung on the wall just over the area where his equipment was placed. Once a female friend complained that she felt the photographs were watching her.

"They are," Freedom told her. Later that evening when he'd gone to the bathroom, he returned to find that the woman had taken the pictures down. Freedom said nothing. He simply tossed the woman her clothes and walked out to his car. After about twenty minutes, she realized Freedom wasn't coming back. She got dressed, went out, and found him sitting there. She got in and asked what happened. Freedom said nothing. He just blasted his music and drove the woman back to her apartment. She was yet another woman Freedom would never see or call again.

Freedom spent several hours listening to the tracks he'd laid down the night before. They were weak, but it wasn't his fault. "Can't get blood from a turnip," his grandmother would say. But what he considered weak, record executives and Elum N Nation would consider brilliant.

Freedom ejected the tape from the deck and popped in Phyllis Hyman. "Why did you have to die?" he asked out loud. "We could have made beautiful music," he said to the haunting melodies.

Freedom's cell phone rang, and after a few seconds, just before the call went into voice mail, he found the phone under the pillow he'd briefly slept on.

"Peace," he said.

"I knew you'd be up," his attorney said in her "I bet I was up before you were" voice.

"Hey," Freedom said to Ava.

"So, I been checking into this house thing," she said, changing the subject. "It's available, but it's been tied up in a trust. Fortunately, I happen to know the attorney who's handling it. Believe it or not," she said shyly, "we went to school together."

"Yeah?" Freedom said.

"Yes," she replied. "He's one of those 'I'm-not-really-from-the-hood-so-there's-no one-for-me-to-give-anything-back-to' brothers."

"Sounds like your type," Freedom teased. "But seriously, when do I move in?"

"From what my research tells me," she told him, "I'm going to have to do some fancy dancing. I'll do what I can to get you inside to see it quickly. And then you can see for yourself exactly *why* it's empty. I'm telling you, Freedom, the place is *haunted*."

"Enough with that haunted madness."

"Alright, but when the ghosts come and get you, don't say I didn't warn you," she added.

"Girl, the only thing haunting me is the thought of *you* being with me."

"Right," Ava said, and hung up. She knew that her phone would immediately ring and that Freedom would be on the other end demanding that she end the conversation properly.

"You better tell me 'Peace' before I fire you," he would always say.

Today would not be any different.

7

a private matter

> History. Lived not written, is such a thing
> not to understand always, but to marvel.
> —*J. California Cooper*

*M*r. Campbell, please," Ava said on the phone to Charles's assistant.

"May I ask who's calling?" she asked.

Ava hated this question. She always wanted to say, "No, you may not." Either your boss is in or he's not. *Screen the call after you know who's on the other end,* she thought to herself. Instead, she answered politely. "Yes, you may. This is Ava Vercher. V-e-r-c-h-e-r." She spelled the name slowly. It was an odd name, but that's why she liked it. Ava knew that calls were returned and new appointments were kept because the name "Vercher" didn't sound like the name of a black attorney from Brooklyn. Vercher was her sister Myrna's last name. Myrna had raised Ava after their mother died when Ava was only five and just starting school. There was a thirteen-year gap between Ava and her sister, and although Myrna was young, she was a good mother to Ava. On the first day of school after their mother had died Ava saw the way the teacher looked at her and then at her very fair-skinned sister.

"Why is your child's last name different from yours?" Ava was named Brown after her black father. Myrna was a Vercher like her white father. In a very certain tone, Ava's sister told the teacher that it was a private matter. Young Ava loved the sound of that phrase "private matter."

"That means it's our business," Myrna would tell her little sister later. From then on, whenever anyone asked Ava something she didn't want to answer or something she didn't know the answer to, she would say, "It's a private matter." The answer worked well in her life, but she didn't want to be different from her sister, so along with her phrases and mannerisms, Ava took her sister's name.

"I'm calling Mr. Campbell about a property he's researching for me." Ava wanted to add her bra and panty size for the assistant, but decided against it.

"One moment please," the assistant replied.

He's either sleeping with her, or he used to, Ava said to herself once she heard the Muzak playing in her ear. Marvin Gaye's "What's Going On?" had been desecrated. *What is* really *going on?* Ava thought.

"Ava, good to hear from you," Charles said a few minutes

later, and a bit too happily for Ava. "I've done some preliminary work and found out that the house is available, but it's not as reasonable as I thought."

Ava wanted to say, "Look Chucky, you know I knew you when you were called Pee Pee boy," but again, she held her tongue. "Right," she said instead. "Look, I'm gonna be up-front with you because I know you'd do the same for me. My client wants the property, and I want him to have it. But I'm not going to let his wants outshine his needs. Before I even step foot in that haunted hellhole, I want figures—the *real* figures. When can we meet?"

Mr. Charles "Large and In-Charge" Campbell III was taken by surprise. "Um, um, well, I have to look at my calendar," he stammered.

"Calendar, my big butt," Ava said. "Now, you know I don't like to play hardball, because I *am* hardball, so I don't have to play. But for you, homeboy, I will. Meet me at, say, six o'clock, House of Tina. You remember the place?" Ava asked.

She knew that Charles was familiar with the neighborhood Chinese restaurant-nightclub that she'd forced him to meet her at before. Several years before, when they'd first reconnected, Charles said that he would prefer to do business over dinner, and he rather gallantly allowed her to pick the place. But he wasn't too thrilled when she chose a place in their old Brooklyn neighborhood. He'd planned on dazzling Ava with his new, im-proved self. Instead, he regressed into a grown-up version of Chucky. Now she was forcing that regression again.

"Can't we, I mean, is it possible for us to meet someplace else, someplace more—"

"White?" Ava interrupted. "No. I have to do some volun-teer work at the shelter around the corner from there, so

HOT"—as she alone called House of Tina—"is the best I can do. You want to get rid of that albatross, don't you?"

"Fine," Charles said.

"Then, six o'clock it is," she added. "Oh, by the way, Charles, bring your dancing shoes. It's Ladies' Night."

Charles was fuming, but Ava was smiling, exposing the beautiful gap between her two front teeth that Charles Campbell III had fallen in love with long ago, when he was still called Chucky.

8

memories of long ago

We wish to plead our own cause.

—*Marcus Garvey*

The house on Tubman Terrace played back memories like a stereo programmed on repeat. The memories of its inhabitants rushed in like waves on a shore. Each one came in farther and farther until they had to recede and start over again. The memories were always the same, but sometimes, depending on the tide, they were more and more intense. At such times, the memories were close enough and loud enough to be felt by people outside the house, and anyone who happened to be near the house on Tubman Terrace would be carried away with those tides.

When they returned, they would not be themselves. Once people were touched by those tides they were changed forever.

Years before, in the twenties, a gangster had moved into the house. A month later he was found dead. The police, lacking any evidence of forced entry, ruled the death a suicide, but the folks who worked for him knew otherwise.

Tonight the memories played loudly.

Ngozi awoke hoping this all had been a dream. It was not. Cold water had been thrown at him with all the fervor of a sharpened spear. The water hit him like thousands of tiny knives meant to kill, but intending to do so slowly.

"Get up, you lazy dog," the voice of the pale man said.

Ngozi could not understand the words, but his spirit could interpret the hatred. He pulled himself upward and tried to shake off his pain. His body ached in places he hardly ever thought about. From the pit of his stomach to the lower part of his neck, he felt as if he'd been sliced in the same manner that one would open the prize of a difficult hunt. His wrist and ankles bled from the constant pulling they had received on board the ship, but the greatest pain was in his heart. He felt an emptiness he had experienced once long ago.

Years before, he'd fallen from a tree and hit the ground so hard his breath left his body. But very quickly his breath was restored, so he childishly climbed the tree again. Now it was as if he was falling and hitting the ground over and over again, so quickly that the life force could not come back, so quickly that he couldn't remember his life before this moment at all. He wished for death, but Ngozi knew that death could only come when he was ready, or at a point when he was doing his descendants more harm than they could ever overcome. This was the gracefulness of his God, to allow entrance into the next life when the spirit was prepared. He realized all that he had been: son, husband, brother, warrior. And he thought of everything that he no longer was.

Ngozi stood an entire foot and a half taller than the man who hated him, but the pale man's hatred loomed larger. Ngozi thought of the proverb his father spoke. "When you meet an envious man on the road and you pass him by, if the kindness in your heart is not as great as the hatred in his, you will become envious and full of hatred also. The man who is more committed to his feelings is the man who wins in the battle of spirits." Ngozi knew that the pale man was winning in the battle of spirits. And although Ngozi had reason to feel hatred toward the man, Ngozi had not been taught to hate; all he could feel for this man was pity. The pain in Ngozi's heart was not wild enough to push forth the poison of hate. It would be many generations before his children's children would be strong enough to walk among men who harbored enough hatred to enslave others. Once their hatred matched that of their captor, they would have forgotten the proverb that taught their ancestors that the only weapon that can do battle with hatred is the weapon of love and peace.

9

between the beats

> When you walk in purpose,
> you collide with destiny.
> —*Pastor Ralph Buchanan*

*F*reedom left his place in Brooklyn and drove to Manhattan. He had to meet a film producer who wanted some of his work for a movie. During the first part of his drive, Freedom felt like he should change his name. *I had more freedom when I was just Harry Hudson who cleaned banks after school when he was a kid,* he reflected.

He turned off at the next exit to go to the office where his appointment was. When he did, he saw that he was near the house on Tubman. He was already late, but chose to drive by the house and take in the fine architectural details. As he slowed to a stop, the same flicker of lights he'd seen last time danced in the upper window. *Must be my eyes,* Freedom thought to himself as he closed them. When he did, he heard the beating of a distant drum. Between the beats, Freedom could hear the sound of waves crashing into a shoreline. Had it not been for the sound of the water, Freedom would have assumed that the drum sounds were coming from one of his soon-to-be white neighbors, trying to connect with the spirit of Harlem. But Freedom was startled and somewhat frightened by the sound and when his eyes fluttered open, the sound disappeared and the dancing lights were gone. "Whoo," Freedom said out loud. "I need to stop listening to Ava's madness. She got me hearing *and* seeing things."

Freedom laughed uneasily and pulled away from the curb. Just as he did, a small boy, who looked to be no more than five years old, darted across the street in front of his car. Freedom swerved and slammed on his brakes, barely missing the boy. Freedom immediately looked for the child's parents so he could give them a good piece of his mind. But he didn't see anyone at all. He turned to yell at the kid, but couldn't find him either.

All of this had taken place in a matter of seconds, but the street was large enough to take longer than that to cross. Feeling cheated, Freedom cursed the air instead. If he had bothered to look in his rearview mirror, he would have seen the child, or rather, the spirit of the child in the backseat of his SUV. Johnny, as he had been known in life, had his hand over his mouth to muffle the sound of his laughter. Knowing that he could not go beyond this street until he'd made a connection, as Freedom pulled off, the little boy reluctantly left the car.

"See you later, alligator," Johnny said to the back of Freedom's head, and then was gone.

10

the office fling

*A*va was filling out her last intake form at the women's shelter where she volunteered. Even though the place was full, compared to summer when this place would be overflowing, this was a slow period. Ava quickly learned the effects heat had on the human temper. In her first summer there she'd more than served her time as a volunteer. The shelter had been swamped—violence went up with the temperature. In between checking women in she gave legal counsel to women who couldn't afford it. Her friend Meredith, who was good at getting folks to volunteer, had convinced Ava to work at the shelter. Ava often wondered how she did it. Meredith was mild mannered and humble, but when it came to community work, she was a warrior.

When Ava began volunteering at the shelter, she was surprised to find out that very few battered women were ready to divorce their abusers. She was even more surprised by the number of women who went back to their men, only to return to the shelter a few months later.

Meredith told her, "This is why we need you."

"I'm a lawyer. I should be giving legal advice," she told her friend.

"What's even more important," Meredith said, "is that they see a strong sister who has made it and can take care of herself. They need to see that you exist."

Ava thought about this now as she sat in the closet that had been converted to an office. "Yeah, if the Harvard boys could see me now," she said to no one.

Although Ava did not regret her decision to work for herself and her people, she often wondered what her life would have been like had she chosen a different path. She wondered if she'd be married with kids, or simply lonely and chasing someone else's dreams. Ava couldn't admit to herself that she was lonely, so she decided that her single life was a choice. She was certain that she'd rather be miserable alone than wrapped up in some brother's madness.

But in quiet moments, Ava knew that her real fear was in surrendering herself to just the *idea* of love. She thought of love as an ocean in which you either get lost or drown. Ava, always the practical one, preferred solid ground, and the single life in which there was no possibility of abuse or arguments. No one to leave the toilet seat up or care that she had left it down. In her heart she wished for balanced love, but in her life she settled for what she knew she could control.

Ava looked at her watch and saw that it was already twenty minutes to six in the evening. She wanted to be at House of Tina before Charles. Ava filled out the rest of the forms in the stack that sat before her and dashed into the bathroom for a quick freshening up. She checked her reflection in the mirror and then dabbed a bit of frankincense and myrrh behind her ears, on her temples and wrists, and left for her appointment.

The weather was mild, so Ava walked the few blocks to House of Tina. Once there, Ava was greeted by Tina herself.

"You not been here long time," Tina said in her Chinese-Brooklyn accent. Ava stifled the desire to laugh that always came whenever she spoke to Tina.

"I know. I've been real busy," Ava replied.

"You too busy for your soul sister?" Tina asked. Tina was married to a brother that no one had ever seen in person. The story was that he lived somewhere down South and that Tina visited him on holidays. This was just one of the many mysteries surrounding Tina.

Tina sashayed her tiny body around Ava's and escorted her to what she thought of as the best seat in the house, placed at the center of the restaurant. Tables on the dinner side of the restaurant-nightclub were decorated with bright pink tablecloths topped off with red glass candles, which Tina lit for Ava. "You want order now, or you wait for some fine soul brother?" Tina asked.

"I'm waiting," Ava said, "but I don't know how fine he is."

Tina laughed. "You so funny, soul sister," she said as she moved on. "I send my best girl to wait on you," she shot back. Ava took in the familiar surroundings. She could see the dance floor from where she was. DJ Donny was already setting up.

"What's up, sis?" he asked between movements as he unloaded what was known to be the best record collection in all of Brooklyn.

"You got it, my brother," Ava answered.

"Gots to be a good night if you up in here," he said.

"And you know that," she added. Ava looked over the menu even though she knew what she would order. Tina's specialty was chicken and ribs, Chinese style, but she made a mean pot of greens, too. Ava always ordered the vegetable plate and vegetable fried rice. Ava looked around to see if Charles had managed to slip in, and instead she caught her reflection in the smoky block mirrors that covered the back wall. Against the wall was a big wicker chair where scantily clad women would later gather to have their picture taken. *You know you're ghetto if* . . . Ava said to herself and laughed. Bamboo fencing hung from the ceiling to give what Tina thought was an outdoor, island feeling. Ava knew Charles definitely thought this place was ghetto, and in truth, so did Ava. But she liked ghetto as much as Charles liked boring art openings. *To each his own,* Ava thought.

House of Tina was still somewhat empty, but folks were trickling in with hopes of getting a good spot. In a couple of more hours, the joint would be jumping. Ladies' Night started early, and folks who had worked hard honest jobs as well as those who had easy and not so honest jobs would pile in to get their groove on. Ava's cell phone rang, and she immediately suspected it was Charles.

"Yes?" she said into the phone as she looked at Charles's office number on her caller ID.

"Hello Ava, this is Charles," the absent attorney said.

Ava mouthed the word, "Duh," but said, "Hey, you're usually more prompt than this." She checked her watch. "It's— wow, my brother, you're an entire thirty minutes late. You keep this up, and people will be saying you operate on CP time. You're going to make it, aren't you?" she asked.

Charles sighed. "Yes, of course. I couldn't get out of my office on time, and now I'm stuck in traffic," he said, not realizing that Ava knew exactly where he was calling from. "It'll be another say thirty, forty minutes before I can get there," he added.

Ava thought before she responded. She didn't want to say anything that would make Charles play hard in their business negotiations, but she still wanted to let him know that her time was important. "Fine, I understand," she said calmly. "Can I order for you?"

Charles didn't respond right away, and just when Ava thought that maybe he wouldn't, he said, "Ah, yes, that would be nice. Surprise me."

"Dinner will be on the table when you get here. And by the way, Charles, tell your secretary I said hello," she said just before ending the call.

Charles cursed when he remembered that most cell phones were now equipped with caller ID. He adjusted his tie and ran from his office, barely saying goodnight to the secretary who hoped to be more than just an office fling.

11

the summons

> What ain't done in this life,
> has to get done in the next.
>
> — *Caroline Freeman*

Ngozi had been in this strange land long enough to understand some things. Although he could now grasp the meaning of the words these people spoke, he could not comprehend the motivation for their actions. He was not alone in this madness. There was Stabo, his sister's husband, and many, many others who looked like him but were born in this strange place. They spoke the same language as the pale people, but they had some of Ngozi's ways. Like the way they jumped the broom for marriage or hung palms over the door when someone died. Still they looked upon him with suspicion. Ngozi could sense that they were ill at ease whenever he was present. He knew that their inability to connect had a great deal to do with the fact that there was no drum.

Everyone was worked hard. So hard that it made no sense to Ngozi. It was as if the pale people didn't care whether the people who looked like him lived or died. If they died, who would do their work? Back in his country, some of Ngozi's people had servants, but they were not treated in this manner.

Ngozi wondered how the warriors who had captured him would feel if they'd known the horror they had sold him into. Ngozi was certain that the blood of the lost would be on the heads of those traitors for generations to come. He saw in his spirit that they would be forced to war among themselves. No leader would ever find peace. One would be ousted for another in a bloody takeover, and the cycle would continue again. Plague and famine would rule their lands, and they would find little relief. This would be the price for selling their brothers into slavery, death with no release. But those who bought and worked the enslaved, they would pay an even greater price. They would do to one another what they had done to those they enslaved.

Ngozi noticed many differences between himself and the other blacks. His spirit was still in his homeland. Their spirit was (also) not here, and neither was the drum. Ngozi often wondered about this. The spiritless workers sang beautiful, sad songs as they toiled in the fields. Sometimes they played stringed instruments, and they even danced. The dances, though few and too far in between, were wild and passionate, but they were not the dances he remembered. His dances were not driven by melody. They were led by the raw sound of the beat.

Once, when they were allowed to play music and dance, Ngozi found a bucket and began to play the rhythms he'd grown up with. Suddenly, the dancing changed. It became more collective. Folks who'd been dancing as couples became clusters. Groups formed, and the dancing became frenzied with more energy than Ngozi had ever seen experienced by those who looked like him. He felt more connected than ever before. But as quickly as that connection was made, it was put to an end. Ngozi felt a sharp sting that he'd come to know as the lash. He turned to see the plantation owner standing with a whip ready to come down on him again.

"Boy, we don't 'low no Africa mess round here," he barked.

"He ain't know," one of the older men said. Tom, as he was called, was respected by everyone that worked the fields. Even those who controlled the place had some respect for him.

"He may not know, but he will," the plantation owner said. He beat him until his back was ripped open. Ngozi wondered what he'd done to cause him to be punished as if he'd run away.

Later on, he was told that he'd done just that. After the older women tended to his wounds and his feelings, the old man, Tom, came to him with the wisdom of the fathers.

"He beat you for starting something," he said. "These drum beats ain't allowed here or no place else. It cause folks to feel who they is, who they really is. You know what I'm saying, boy?" the man asked.

Ngozi told him he was not sure of anything.

"That's what they want to beat the life out of you. They know that the drum is special cause it can talk. It can say things they don't understand. That's why it ain't 'lowed. But if you listen close to our songs, you'll hear something. We say one thing, we mean something more. I been watching you," the old man told Ngozi. "Look to me, you think we's bad as they is. But that ain't so. We just trying to live. We won't ever be free, but our children's children, they will. So we have to save ourselves for them. We take this life so they can live. Don't you forget that. Play your drum, boy, but play it here," he said, pointing to his heart. "Some day you'll have the drum, and you can pass it on to those who will *think they free, but ain't. You see boy, we know we ain't free, and we know we won't be. But inside, we are free, cause our children, they might be. Hold on for them, and someday you'll bring the drum back."*

Ngozi no longer tried to make sense of his condition. He spent his days in remembrance of the words his mother had spoken to him. He felt the power in them. No one in this place had a drum. No rhythms were played for the birth of a child. Neither did they sound and tell of a death. Instead, his lost brethren sang melodies that were sad and somehow beautiful. Songs that made him weep no matter what the meaning. The songs were born of suffering and sorrow, but without the rhythm of the drum, they could not send the message home.

Ngozi wept for the drum he was to have made and for the son his wife would have but whom he would never see. He wept for his own capture. All these things were connected, for the loss of this drum and his life were a loss for his son and all of his people.

Ngozi vowed that day and every day that followed that he would find a way to bring back the drum.

Remembering this now as he stood in the house on Tubman Terrace, he was saddened because it had taken him centuries to carry out his vow. In his present state of existence, he could see that the drum was not just for his own life, it was also for those who came after. The drumbeat was needed to connect his people from today to those of the past. The separation had gone on for too long. Still he was encouraged. The rhythm of the drum was present, but it had to be put to the right use. Suddenly, Ngozi heard a whisper. "Ye oh Ye Ba Ba. I hear you, Papa." Ngozi knew that he was being summoned.

12

◆

the exploitation
of hip hop

Yo, this is hip hop, ya'll.
—*Lauryn Hill at the
1999 Grammys*

Freedom walked down the corridor of the fancy office building and was greeted inside the double glass doors by what he would say were too many happy white people.

"Hey, how's the music master?" the famous filmmaker who'd requested the meeting asked.

"Yeah, Mr. Baker, I didn't plan to be late, but you know how it goes." Freedom had long ago stopped being sorry. He would occasionally apologize, but that was rare. And he never used the phrase, "I'm sorry." The black man has nothing to be sorry for, Freedom remembered he'd once heard a street-corner prophet say.

"What's up, Mr. Baker?" Freedom asked.

"Call me Scott, please. We're friends here," the filmmaker said. He led Freedom to a conference room filled with more happy white folks and one black man who upon seeing Freedom looked too uncomfortable to be happy.

"Let me introduce you to everyone," Scott said. Freedom's late arrival had bothered the filmmaker. He couldn't decide if the music producer was rude or just uncouth, but either way it didn't matter. Scott planned to use the man's music and discard him just as he had every other artist that had made him rich and famous. He introduced the conference table of "suits," which included representatives from the film division, financial office, creative department, legal affairs, promotions, publicity, and marketing. Everyone had an assistant present. Freedom felt that the only person missing was someone from the janitorial staff.

"We've all stayed late to accommodate you and to let you see how important this project is to us here," Scott said.

"Great," Freedom told them. "So like I said before, what's up?"

"Well, I like that, Freedom. I see you're a man who gets right down to business." The room was full of smiles and heads nodding in agreement. "I'm not sure if you're aware of this or not," Scott said, "but in the late sixties, early seventies, when this country was in a social uproar, a time when I was very much— what's the expression? 'Down for the cause,' yeah, that's it— most of the industry ignored the struggle, and they suffered for it."

Freedom had heard this pitch style before. He didn't like being in a room full of happy white folks any more than he liked being given a history lesson by one of them.

"MGM," Scott continued, "was about to sell Dorothy's shoes when Gordon Parks saved their lily white asses with *Shaft* and *Shaft's Big Score*."

Freedom wanted to say, "Just get to the deal." He couldn't stand player hating, and here sat Mr. Clean himself, calling the folks who made *The Wizard of Oz*, which he loved, lily white. They were white, but so was Baker. And from what Freedom could see, he was way past white. In fact, he was transparent. Freedom had his own rating system for white folks. There was white, real white, almost white, which he used for uptight blacks, and transparent. The last category was where he placed people like Baker and William F. Buckley Jr.

"Yo, "Over the Rainbow" had mad lyrics," Freedom said.

"Right," Scott said, not following Freedom's thought. "What we're getting to is the fact that once again, we are in a period of change. Look at music. What kind of music sells more than any other?" Before waiting for anyone to answer, Scott continued, "Country and hip hop and Latin, or Hispanic, depending on which part of the country you're from," he said, evoking chuckles from all but Freedom. "The music of the people, the forgotten underclass, *la clase baja*. The voice of pain and sorrow. And the film industry has once again ignored the signs of change. That's where we come in," Scott said, about to make the point Freedom had been waiting for. Scott felt that he was truly connecting to Freedom. Freedom felt Scott was being condescending.

"We intend to do what Brother Parks did in the seventies," Scott continued.

"You mean Blaxploitation?" Freedom asked.

"Well, that's the label it's been given," Scott said, "but we don't intend to *exploit*, rather we want to *expose*." As if struck by some brilliant wand, he added, "Black Expos-ation."

The room began to buzz with support of the phrase that Freedom saw as just plain wack. "Right, whatever," he said. "What do you need me for? Am I the black part?" he said only half joking.

At first the room was silent. Then after Scott smiled, they all laughed.

"Great line. Can I use that?" the lone black man from the legal department asked.

"Sure, Money, just give me credit," Freedom said mockingly.

Scott allowed the laughter to build but then calmed the room. "We have a loose concept," he said, "but from what I hear, *you're* just the man we need to pull this baby together."

Freedom wanted to say, "Solid, Mack," but he held back.

"With your musical genius and contacts, we can make a lot of money together, and at the same time 'expose' the masses to the real side of your hip-hop world." When Scott said the word "expose," he raised his hands and used the tacky two-finger gesture to indicate that the word was in quotes.

Freedom wanted to hit the man, but he also wanted to make a movie. "So you want to make a movie around my music, but you don't have a script. And you don't have any actors, right?" he asked.

"Well, we're looking at Halle Berry as one of the lead rap-pers," someone from the creative department said.

Scott shot the man a look, and everyone sat silently. "We'd like you to lead the way on this," Scott said through clenched teeth.

"What do you have?" Freedom asked.

"We have the studio and the backing to make and distribute the film," Scott said smiling. "All the backing you need."

Freedom stood and grabbed one of the unopen bottles of Evian water that sat in front of him. "I'll think about it," he said as he started toward the door.

"Great," Scott said, dumbfounded. "So I'll hear from you when?" he asked.

Freedom turned and smiled and said, "When I call," and used the same in quotes gesture Scott had used earlier. Once again, all conference room held back their laughter until Scott indicated that he, too, thought Freedom had made a funny.

"Really," Freedom said, "let me talk with my attorney, and I'll call you, alright?" And then he left.

Scott looked around the room and nodded. "Well, I think that went real well, don't you?" Of course, everyone agreed.

Back in the house on Tubman Terrace, the spirit memory, Johnny, had been called back inside. The house had been inhabited by spirit memories for years and had become a holding place for memories waiting for the Gathering of Souls, a time when spirits could tell their story to connect with the living. The memories were difficult for them to relive, but they had to be experienced and told so that the living could find peace. It wasn't the spirit memories that were restless. It was the living, and because Harlem, New York, had been the port of entry as well as the dwelling place for millions of restless black folks, Harlem pulled the memories like few other places. This particular house was like lots of abandoned places, but because of its history, it had an even greater pull.

Johnny wanted to play kick ball, but the man with the drum and the funny name said that he had to come inside. "You're not my father," Johnny snapped.

"No," Ngozi said calmly. "Your father killed you, and I would not have done such a thing."

Johnny's attitude returned to sorrow. That was the reason he left the house in the first place. Johnny had been remembering his own death, and the memories were more intense than usual.

"Things will change soon," said Ngozi, the man with the drum.

"I hope so," Johnny whispered.

"They will. They have to for the sake of our souls and for his soul, too."

In the corner listening was the spirit memory of the woman that Freedom had called Grand. "Don't worry," she said. "He'll do the right thing. I know he will."

13

pain before pleasure

If you don't like my peaches,
don't shake my tree.
—*Blues song*

*T*rue to his word, Charles appeared within forty minutes, albeit somewhat flushed. He could barely look Ava in the eye. "Sorry I'm late," he mumbled.

"It's cool," Ava replied.

The waitress appeared with a tray full of food. There were ribs, chicken wings, shrimp fried rice and greens, along with Ava's vegetable plate. "The last time we were here you didn't eat, but I'm not letting you off tonight."

"Looks really good, and I'm famished." Charles was actually licking his lips.

"I figured you would be hungry," Ava said, grinning. Charles blushed but regained composure quickly. Ava knew that brothers like Charles didn't take too well to being caught in their mess, but he was too interested in the food to be bothered. At first he approached the ribs like he'd never seen them before, but quickly reacquainted himself with the kind of food he had tried to forget. After one bite, Charles was wondering why he ever liked sushi and tiny decorative plates of haute cuisine. He ate like a man on a mission. Ava wanted to laugh, but she was also thinking that there might be hope for Mr. Charles after all. She called the waitress over and asked for more ribs and chicken. Charles had barely looked up but managed to add, "More greens, too, please."

Now Ava laughed. "You might make it after all," she said, sharing her thoughts. By now DJ Donny was spinning his disks. He'd started slow for the supper crowd, playing jazz tunes and then eased into old school.

She noticed how happy Charles looked and made a mental note to hold more of her meetings at House of Tina. Charles finally looked up and wiped his hands. As if suddenly remembering why he was there, he said, "Oh yeah, about the house." His thought was interrupted when he saw that there was one more chicken wing left.

"Go for it, brother," Ava told him.

Without missing a beat, Charles grabbed the wing and continued his conversation. "The house is tied up in trust, but it will be pretty easy to handle. It's owned by a family that never lived in it. The house originally belonged to the grandfather, and he left it to the children of the son he referred to in his will as 'that no good son of mine.' The grandchildren took one look at the location and wanted to have nothing to do with it. They'd tried to sell it, but one of the siblings wanted a larger share of the inheritance and wouldn't allow the sale." Charles whispered this last bit of information as if it were his own family's secret.

"Yeah, we had that same problem," Ava said mockingly. "My grandfather left some bills, and now everybody is fighting over who's going to have to pay them."

Charles managed a weak laugh, though he didn't really see the connection. "They want a lot of money for the property even though it's in disrepair," he said. "Apparently, they've kept up on all of the recent development in the area so they figure that the house is worth twice what they were originally asking."

Ava eyed Charles curiously. "No doubt the white media and real estate brokers are keeping this greedy family appraised of all of the Harlem goings-on," Ava said.

"I see. As always, you've done your homework."

"Yes, and I know about the mall Disney is building and the fact that the parallel block is also now in transition. But none of that has anything to do with this particular house. What's really the deal with this house? Is it really haunted?" Ava asked, as if she was asking about something as common as taxes.

Charles responded in the same manner. "Well, I haven't seen anything myself, but to tell you the truth, that place gives me the willies. The family sees the rumor about the house being haunted as gossip generated by potential buyers, but they haven't even been inside."

"Do you have any history on the source of the haunting?" Ava asked.

"I've checked old newspapers, but I couldn't really find anything. Supposedly," Charles said, "there are several ghosts. Sort of like a poltergeist thing. Some say it's the original owners, but I don't think that's the case." Charles paused and looked as if he wanted to say more but had decided not to.

"There's something you're not telling me," Ava discerned.

"Well, I know this was improper, but I told my grandmother about the place. She's sort of a, well . . . my grandmother is different. When I told her I had a client who was interested in that house, she got spooked and told me not to deal with it."

"You know how old folks are," Ava said.

Ava remembered the woman, Miss Dora, who used to visit from somewhere down South every two or three years when they were still children. She was the first woman she'd ever seen who smoked a pipe. "She surely was strange," Ava muttered. Then she thought of how strange it was that two well-educated attorneys were having a normal conversation about what they believed to be a haunted house. *Maybe Charles is more in touch with the hood than he pretends to be,* she thought to herself. "Bottom line, Charles, what do they want?" Ava asked, getting right to the money.

"They're asking five hundred thousand," Charles said without blinking.

"Right," Ava said, laughing, "and I'm going to tell my client that he should pay just that."

Charles sat silently for a moment and finally said, "I'll try to get them down to four," as if it would be the most difficult thing he'd ever done.

"No, brother, we'll give the greedy tribe two fifty, but if they piss me off, it'll be two."

Now Charles laughed. "Look girl, we aren't playing hide-and-seek in the old neighborhood anymore."

Ava raised her eyebrows in surprise. Until now, she wasn't sure if Charles even remembered their childhood games.

"Yeah, and if we were," she said, "you'd be caught."

"Are you forgetting that I always found you?" Charles asked slyly.

Ava blushed. In fact, she had forgotten. Until now, she had also forgotten that Charles had had a crush on her that was so intense that it had almost been an obsession. She never liked it when her girlfriends teased her. "Pee Pee boy likes Gappy. Pee Pee boy likes Gappy," they'd say, calling them both by their nicknames. For the first time that evening, Ava was speechless.

But just as she was wondering what to say, she caught Lil' Man in the mirror strolling over in her direction. Rick James's "Fire and Desire" was playing, and Lil' Man was singing it loudly, using his beer bottle as a microphone. "And then I laid eyes on you. It was pain before plea-e-sure," he wailed. "Hey Miss Fine Thang, when you gonna break down and have dinner with me?" he said to Ava but staring at Charles and daring him to speak. Lil' Man was about six foot five and all of 450 pounds. He had beautiful, smooth, jet-black skin and a shoulder-length bob to match. Lil' Man always dressed monochromatically, right down to the shoes. Today he was outfitted in lime green, complete with matching alligator shoes. "You can at least give me a dance," he said, pulling at Ava, still staring at Charles like he was just a table decoration.

"Sure, Lil' Man, but not right now. I'm doing some business."

"Humph," Lil' Man snorted. "He don't look like he thinking 'bout no business to me."

Charles didn't bother to defend himself. He recognized Lil' Man as his childhood bully, but Lil' Man hadn't recognized him.

Ava was aware of this and decided to have some fun. "Lil' Man, you know Charles. We used to call him Chucky. He lived upstairs from you."

Lil' Man leaned back to get a better view. "That's you, Pee Pee boy?" he asked in disbelief. "Damn, man, you actually grew up. I thought you'd a drowned in your own pee. I used to hear your mama whipping your ass for peeing." Lil' Man raised an imaginary belt and swung with each syllable. "If-I-told-you-once-I-told-you-twice. Stop-pee-ing-on-my-fur-ni-ture." Lil' Man howled with laughter.

Ava's plan had gone too far. She was embarrassed for Charles. She suddenly realized that she needn't be.

Charles stared Lil' Man right in the eyes. "I see you grew up too, Lil' Man, or should I say blew up?"

Ava had been sipping her water trying to figure out a way to get rid of Lil' Man. Drinking water at that moment had not been a good idea. She laughed and watched as the contents of her mouth sprayed Lil' Man's green silk suit. "Ooo, I'm so sorry, Lil' Man," she said between snickers.

"It's not your fault," Charles told her. "You couldn't have missed the Jolly Green Giant if you'd tried."

Lil' Man, who had previously been all mouth, was now

reduced to silence. "I was just messing with you, Chucky. You ain't gotta be so mean," Lil' Man moaned.

"Then don't start nothing you can't finish, big boy, or Lil' Man, or whatever it is you go by. And by the way," Charles added, "isn't your real name Herbert Black? I remember *you* used to cry when the teachers called us by our last name first. Black Herbert."

This was all Lil' Man could take. "Look, man, I came in here to have a nice time. I wasn't trying to start no trouble. I know when I'm beat."

Charles was on a roll and was enjoying the fact that he was finally bullying his bully. "How would you know when you're beat? How could you feel it through all of that fat and green? Here, you left your microphone," he said, raising the beer bottle Lil' Man had set down.

Lil' Man was already at the door when Ava finally managed to say, "Alright, Charles. Alright, that's enough."

"Well, you know what they say," he said. "Don't start nothing, won't be nothing."

"And just when did *you* learn to play the dozens?" Ava asked.

"You know, I picked up a lil' something here and there. I'm on a roll," he said loudly.

"Great, then roll yourself over to your office and get the key to that house. I want to see what I'm bidding on."

"I thought you told me to put on my dancing shoes."

"Look, Charles, don't let the greens get to your head. Next thing I know, you'll be growing an afro. Do you have the key or not?" she persisted.

Charles was all teeth as he reached into his front jacket pocket and pulled out a key.

"Girl, I got it right here. It's getting late, but if you want to chance it, I'm game."

Now Ava smiled. When she did, Charles asked, "How 'bout a game of hide-and-seek?"

"Come on, boy, you've had too much to eat" was all she could manage.

14

• ◆ •

things that go bump

During the ride up to Tubman Terrace, Charles and Ava barely spoke. The playfulness they had enjoyed back at House of Tina's was replaced by a feeling of apprehension. Both wondered why they were going to the house after dark. From what they had heard, daylight wasn't any less threatening, but at least they'd be able to *see* the things they feared.

"Is the electrical power on?" Ava finally asked.

"Uh, yes, I'm sure it is. It's required by the new neighbor-hood association in case of an emergency. I think it just makes the neighbors feel safer," Charles said.

"Good," Ava said. "I don't want to fall through some damn hole in the floor because your people haven't taken care of their business."

"Do you kiss your mother with that mouth?" Charles asked.

"As a matter of fact, I do. If you recall," Ava said, "I got this mouth from Myrna."

Charles smiled and remembered the cussing he would hear when Ava's sister, Myrna, had to come and get her after the streetlights were on. "Those were the days when authority fig-ures ruled," Charles said.

As they pulled up to the curb in front of the house on One hundred thirty-eighth Street and Tubman Terrace, Ava became more and more nervous. Charles parked the car, turned to her, and asked, "Remind me: Why are we doing this?"

"Because I want to, uh, need to," she corrected, "see what I'm bidding on. It's my responsibility to my client. This piece of shit may not be worth fifty cents."

"Yes," Charles agreed, "but why can't we do this tomorrow?"

"Well," Ava said, "we could go back to Tina's and get our groove on. I'm sure by now Lil' Man is tore up from the floor up and probably drunk enough to call you some real names."

"That sounds good," Charles said sarcastically, "but I'll take a rain check. How about tomorrow? I haven't eaten that well in a long time. Truth is," he added, "I'm wondering why it took you to bring me back to my old hood."

Ava ignored the direction the conversation was moving in.

"Tomorrow sounds fine," she said. "I'll just have to check my calendar."

Charles laughed. "Well, are we or aren't we?" Charles asked.

"Yes, dinner sounds fine," Ava told him.

"No, Gappy," he said, using the nickname Ava hadn't heard since she was a teenager, "are we going in or not?"

There was a part of Ava that wanted to scream, "No," but she fought the urge and allowed her curiosity to win out.

It was a decision she would come to regret.

15

the Gathering

When one is on the
soil of one's ancestors,
most anything can come.
—*Jean Toomer*

*T*hey're coming," Johnny said excitedly so all could hear.

"But he's not with them," a voice said.

"He'll soon come," a third voice added.

"They are still our people," someone chimed.

"Speak for yourself," the memory of a woman hissed. "I had no
people," she said.

"Whose fault is it that you were just a broke-down whore?" young

Johnny said. Seeing his sweet image, it was hard to believe that the words had come from his five-year-old mouth. His spirit, however, was much, much older.

"I was never broke down," the woman responded.

"That will be enough," Ngozi said, standing on the huge staircase in front of the others. "This is the beginning of what was to be. We gather for those who are forgotten, those who are lost at sea, and those who are lost to their own children. We gather to tell our stories with the hopes that one day they will be heard. The sea is full, the tide is high. Johnny," the man said, "tonight we will hear your tale."

Johnny smiled and pushed through the crowd of spirit memories. He was about to speak when they heard a key push through the chambers of the lock. They stood on one side of the door in anticipation and Charles and Ava stood the same way on the other.

"After you," Charles said once the lock had been disengaged.

"Naw, after you," Ava returned. "Haven't you heard in African culture, the man goes first to check for danger? Besides, age before beauty."

Charles laughed, but he was not feeling giddy at all. He pushed open the door and felt the wall for the light switch.

"Can't your clients afford to keep one light on?" Ava whispered.

"Woman, why are you whispering?" Charles asked. "You afraid you might wake the dead?"

"Something like that," she said just a bit louder.

"Ah, here we are," Charles said, feeling the switch. He flipped it into the up position. A light so bright flashed that he was temporarily blinded. He adjusted his eyes and looked at Ava. "What the——?" Before he could finish, a huge mahogany staircase became visible. There standing in front of them was the Gathering. The spirit memories of beings long gone were gathered together. They had come together out of the necessity to communicate with the next generation. Some were old when they made their transition, others were young. Some were dressed in clothing that dated back to the 1800s. Some had afros. One even looked like a pimp from a bad movie. There was a woman with a bloody newborn. No one made a sound. All of them were black. All had a message to convey.

There in the front of the group stood a very dark man holding a drum. Next to him stood the young boy. He looked as if he were about to speak, but before he did, Ava let out a scream that caused Charles to scream, too. The lights flashed again, and the staircase was empty.

What happened next was like the punch line of the black comedian's joke about the difference between blacks and whites in a haunted house. "White folk go into a big, abandoned house, the chandelier falls, and they say, 'Honey, let's look at the bedroom.' Black folks, in the same situation say, 'Baby, let's get the hell out of here.'" Ava no longer questioned how black Charles was. He reached the door before she did, and in no time they were back outside and in the car he had opened by remote.

16

visitation of spirits

> When indigenous people talk about spirit,
> they are basically referring to the
> life force in everything.
>
> —*Sobonfu Somé*

Freedom walked into House of Tina, his attorney's favorite spot, and tried to figure out why she liked it. *There's more jheri curls in here than all of Detroit and L.A. combined,* he said to himself. Freedom recognized the DJ and made his way over to say hello. Before he could, Donny was announcing his presence over the mike.

"We got big Freedom in the house, the phattest producer of

hip-hop music in the WO-RLD. Big Freedom, big Freedom. Say yo, yo, yo big Freedom."

Women looked at Freedom through weaves and extensions. Brothers gave him high fives and acted like he was an old friend. "So much for keeping a low profile," he said as he reached the DJ.

"What's up, baby?" Donny said.

"You seen Ava?" Freedom said, getting right to the point. Freedom had known and admired Donny for years. In the DJ world Donny was something of a legend. In the eighties, he could have played in the big hot clubs, but he chose to stay in the hood. "I have what I need. I like my job and the people I work with. I make folks happy. So what more do I need?" he'd say. What he never said, and what no one knew, was that he was House of Tina's mystery man. Donny was Tina's husband.

"Hey, you ain't got time to at least say hello, Harry?" Donny said, forcing Freedom to be respectful.

"Sorry, man, I got too much on my mind, you know how it is."

"Yeah, and I know how it should be, too," Donny responded. "Ava was here for dinner. You know you can't miss that fine queen."

"Yeah, yeah. You know how long ago she left?" Freedom always liked to have as much information as possible so he could challenge Ava later concerning her whereabouts.

"She left about an hour ago maybe."

"Thanks, man," Freedom said. "Yo, I'll catch you."

"Hold up, Freedom," Donny yelled. "Check this tape and tell me what you think."

"Alright," Freedom relented.

"Don't let me hear it on none of that rap shit either," Donny yelled. Freedom held up a black power salute and pushed through the crowded dance floor. He got to his car and dialed his attorney's number. He knew if he didn't do what he'd come to do and leave, he would have about twenty homemade tapes, most from wannabe performers. They were usually bad, but if he didn't take them, he'd be accused of selling out. If he did take them, he ran the risk of being accused of stealing or sucking someone's flavor. Freedom just wanted to find Ava.

Ava and Charles were both trying to determine what it was they had seen, but neither said a word. They were startled by the sound of Ava's cell phone ringing and it was as if they'd been brought back from a time before telephones existed. Ava looked at the phone, as if trying to remember how to use it. Finally, she hit the appropriate button and put her ear to the receiver.

"Peace, girl," Freedom said before Ava could answer.

"Freedom," she said, "thank God. I need to talk to you."

"Well, I got to talk to you first," Freedom said excitedly. "Guess who I had a meeting with?" he said. Before she could answer, Freedom blurted out "Scott Baker, the film-maker. Hey, I rhymed," he said childishly. "He wants to do a movie based on my music. They say they'll give me whatever I need."

Ava understood the importance of what Freedom was

saying and transitioned into attorney mode. "You had an important meeting, and you didn't call me? Who was there? Did you agree to anything? Did you take notes? Boy, you know what happened the last time you went to a meeting without me!"

Freedom did remember, but he didn't want to. He ended up in a verbal contract that caused Ava to have to pull every trick she'd learned in law school and some she'd learned growing up to free him from the deal.

Freedom sucked his teeth. "Chill, woman. They put on the whole dog and pony show. I didn't agree to anything. As a matter of fact, I told them I had to call you first, and you know I don't take notes, but I got it all up here," he said, pointing to his head as if Ava could see him.

"Well, I want to know all of the details," she said.

"Yo, I'll be paying for that house in cash," Freedom told her.

Ava immediately remembered what had just happened. "That's what I need to talk to you about, Freedom. I just left there, and well . . . that place ain't right. We'll find you something else."

"Girl, get out of here with that madness. So you went over there with the Brooks Brother, huh?"

"How did you—"

Before Ava could finish, Freedom added, "Yeah, took that Negro to eat in the hood, and he took you to my house. You ain't supposed to be up in there with nobody but me," he said only half teasing.

"You went by House of Tina?" Ava said. "Boy, you can't do nothing in the hood without everybody knowing about it."

"True that," Freedom said. "So what's he got that I ain't got?"

Ava almost laughed, but she was still shaken from her experience inside the house. "For one thing, he has that age advantage, and for another, he doesn't order me around and tell me how to do my job."

"Right," Freedom said. "If I was that easy, you wouldn't like me so much."

"Listen, little boy," Ava said smiling, "what time can we meet tomorrow?"

"I want to see the house," Freedom said.

"And I told you to forget it. I'm not playing. This is for real," she told him.

"Look, girl, no house, no movie. And I'm not playing. Every time I go by there, it's like the place is calling me home."

Ava stopped smiling. "I know what you mean, Freedom, but believe me, in this case home is not where the heart is. Listen, Harry," she said, calling him by his given name, "let's talk about this tomorrow."

Freedom only allowed his true elders, those with real age advantage, to call him Harry, and only when they were alone. Ava knew this, so he figured she was upset about something and decided to let it slide. "I'll talk with you tomorrow. By then, I hope you have some sense," he said before he barked, "Peace," and hung up.

"Second time in one night someone called me by my birth name," Freedom said aloud. He thought about it only briefly. Freedom hadn't yet accepted what his grandmother used to tell him. She'd say, "Boy, in life there are no coincidences."

Charles had listened to Ava's conversation and now knew who her client was. He wondered if her client was more than just a client and if their relationship was anything like the one he had with his secretary. Thinking about his secretary reminded him of the images he had seen earlier on the steps of the house, particularly the woman who held the bloody newborn. For now, Charles decided he wanted to go home. He would call his grandmother and find out just what was going on.

Ava had Charles drop her off at her apartment. Since she'd walked to Tina's from the women's shelter earlier that evening, she could pick up her car from the shelter the next day. Once she was home Ava felt a little more at ease. But like a teenager in a bad slash-and-gore movie, she checked her closets and under her bed before she got in it. She thought about a nice hot shower but was immediately reminded of *Psycho*. "Naw, I'll just go to bed dirty," she said out loud. She turned on her television and noticed that almost every network was playing a horror flick. So instead, she turned on the radio and jumped into bed.

The light jazz station was just what she needed to fall into the comfort of sleep, and Gerald Albright's sexy saxophone had her dreaming before she knew it. She always dreamt multiple dreams in rapid succession and Ava had taught herself to remember her dreams, because in that state she was able to work out her incomplete tasks of the day. She'd been doing this for years before she stumbled on an article about lucid dreaming. "So this is what it's called." She had laughed. "Why do people have to make a career out of the stuff that should just come natural?" She allowed herself to slide into a deep state of unconsciousness, not quite asleep, but certainly not awake, and she began to dream.

In the first dream she had successfully convinced a woman to stay at the women's shelter with her three children. In the next, she was present at Freedom's meeting. There she structured a deal that made both of them wealthy. Her third dream was more personal and satisfying. In that dream Lil' Man had proposed marriage while Charles interrupted and told him she was spoken for. When he did, the singer Seal glided into House of Tina and told them both to forget it. "She's mine," he told them in his melodious Afro-British accent.

But it was the last dream that spiraled into a nightmare. In this dream the young spirit memory she had seen at the house earlier took her by the hand and said, "Follow me." It was a request that felt more like a command. The feeling was so disturbing that Ava had to force herself to wake up. It was difficult to do and made her think of the old folks' saying, "A witch is riding your back." That's what they said when you were caught in a dream and couldn't get out. Ava had had this feeling many times and luckily knew what to do. She flexed her toes until she was able to blink her eyes. With eyes fully open, she wished she'd left them closed. For at the foot of her bed sat the young spirit child, Johnny. He was tossing an old can in the air and catching it.

Johnny looked directly at Ava and said, "I thought you'd never get here."

Ava blinked her eyes again, thinking that she was still asleep. "Cut that out, girl," the fifty-year-old spirit that appeared in the form of a five-year-old's body said. "I'm real. What you should be asking yourself is whether or not *you* are." Then, he laughed so wickedly that Ava actually cried. "They'll be no sleep for you tonight. Hasn't anyone ever told you not to walk out on your hosts? It's time for you to hear my story."

17

Grandma's hands

The souls of old folks have
a way of seein' things.
—*Jean Toomer*

Charles walked into his apartment and dialed the familiar number. Charles's grandmother was always up. If he hadn't seen her take naps with his own eyes, he would assume she never slept. His grandmother usually answered her telephone within two or three rings. After the fifth, Charles wondered if maybe she'd started to sleep more since she was getting older. By the seventh ring, he grew anxious and wondered if she was okay.

"Hello," a grumpy voice answered. "This better be good."

"Goober," Charles asked in disbelief, "that you?"

His cousin Tony, a.k.a. Goober because of his peanut-shaped head, had been helping out around his grandmother's house as long as Charles could remember. Goober was a little slow in school, but his grandmother had a tender place for him in her heart, and he was good with his hands.

"Where's Grandma, Goober?" Charles asked.

"Hello, cuz. How are you? Hope everything is good down South. Maybe you can come visit sometime?" Goober said with all the sarcasm Charles had ever heard anybody use. Charles never thought Goober was slow. As a kid, he figured it was an act Goober put on so he could get away with all kinds of stuff.

"Sorry, man, how are you? I was just worried when Grandma didn't answer."

"Maybe you should check your messages before you call people in the middle of the night," Goober said.

Charles looked down and saw that there were messages on his machine, but that was always the case. "Grandma called me?" Charles asked.

"Hello, am I speaking English? They say I'm slow, and you're a genius?!" Goober mocked.

"Okay, let's start again," Charles said slowly. "Where's Grandma?"

"She's not here, or I wouldn't be answering the phone."

"Okay, Goober. Calm down," Charles said. "Where is she?"

"I'm calm," Goober said, " 'cause I know where she is. You the one in trouble messing in things that ain't got nothing to do with you. She told you to stay away from that place, but did you listen? Nooo," he said loudly.

Now Charles was truly spooked. "What did . . . how did you know?" Charles asked as his door buzzer sounded.

"If you want to know where Grandma is, go answer your door," Goober told him and hung up.

It was a good thing he'd been warned; otherwise Charles would have had his second fright of the day. There standing in his doorway was his grandmother, holding the handle of a suitcase on wheels and carrying a bag that smelled like the herbs and roots that filled her house.

"Don't stand there, boy. Get this stuff and tell me everything. Don't leave nothing out. I'm already mad at you for doing what I told you not to."

18

◦—◆—◦

rhythm of the night

You done taken my blues and gone.

—*Langston Hughes*

Freedom drove back to the house on Tubman Terrace. Very few would call this place peaceful, but to Freedom the brownstone offered him a measure of peace. He got out of the car, sat on the steps, and eventually fell asleep. He'd only been asleep for about twenty minutes when a homeless man brought him out of his bliss.

"Not the place to crash, chief. Haven't you heard? This house is haunted," the man said to him.

"It's cool," he said to the man. "I'm buying this place."

The man raised his eyebrows, laughed, and said, "Save your money," and walked off. He didn't even bother to ask Freedom for a dollar.

Freedom shook his head and smiled. "Maybe this place is haunted. Anytime the homeless folk don't ask for money, something ain't right."

But Freedom felt more peaceful than he'd felt in a long, long time and knew beyond doubt that this would be his home. "I don't care what foolishness Ava is trying to pull. This is the spot," he said before getting back into his SUV and driving off to decide which honey would get the pleasure of his company tonight.

"Johnny made contact with that woman," a voice said.

"Walked right through her, and she didn't notice," someone else added.

"They were too busy running out of here," a voice said, laughing.

"I almost got him," the woman with the bloody newborn said.

Ngozi sat down with his drum and played a melody with a rhythm that was truly an honor to his people.

Freedom was somewhere else submerged in the ecstasy of a body whose heart he didn't love. Somewhere in the rhythm of his movements, though, he heard the rhythm of a drum. The woman whose body he rode sounded out her pleasure. Freedom was done, but he could still hear the drum song. He would hardly remember this woman's name, but those rhythms would remain with him forever.

part

two

19

restless lives, restless spirits

> The wicked shall cease from troubling.
> The weary shall be at rest.
>
> —*Job 3:17*

Ava was in a panic unlike any she'd remembered. She'd been through quite a bit in life; her mother had died when Ava was just a small girl. The racism in her upstate New York college town had been almost too much to bear, and law school hadn't been much easier, but by then she'd learned to hold her own. But none of the real-life dangers that she'd been exposed to had ever caused her as much fear as she felt now.

"*My name is Johnny Freeman, which is kind of dumb given that I ain't really free*," the spirit memory said.

Ava just looked at him.

"To which you say, 'Pleased to meet you, Johnny,' " he said.

Ava parted her lips to speak but found that she couldn't.

"Nice place," he said. "Why you ain't got no kids? You like 'em, don't you?"

Still, she couldn't speak.

"Sure you do, you just . . ." He paused, looking for the right words. ". . . Haven't had the time or the right man," he said in a voice that Ava would have sworn came from her. It was her own voice, her own thoughts, but he had spoken them as if they were his.

"How did you do that?" was all that she managed.

"Parlor trick," Johnny said nonchalantly. "I got loads of 'em, but I ain't got that much time. I have to tell you my story 'fore the night is over so somebody will remember me and know that my life counted for something. Otherwise," he continued, "I'm just here, incomplete."

"Why me?" Ava asked.

" 'Cause you restless, and 'cause you here listening."

Ava was confused but couldn't say so.

"It's not hard to understand," Johnny told her. "You have no children, and you've been restless about it. Your anxiety can cause your mind to create all kinds of things," he said and winked. "I need to tell my story so folks like you can learn from the past. You listening. That's real good. Some listen. Most don't. When you listen, my memory can rest and you can look for peace."

And with that, he began his tale.

"I was born in a colored hospital in a colored town. They both *long gone, but they were real. You can check. Town called Whitesville, Alabama. All the blacks lived in Whitesville, but the white folks lived in Browntown. That was somebody's idea of a joke. Ain't funny, is it?"*

Ava slowly shook her head, though she knew she hadn't done it herself.

"I didn't think so either. Anyway, my mama died when I was born. My daddy say I kill her. But he say a lot of mean things. I lived with him and my sister. I don't know what kind of man he was 'fore my mama died. Maybe he was nice then. If he was, wasn't none of that left in him. I was what you smart folks call a precocious child. Always getting into things. I like to see how things work. I was like that from when I first start walking, and that was early, too. They have fancy schools for kids like me now. They say kids like that can grow up and invent all kinds of things. Maybe I would've done that, too."

Johnny paused and stared at nothing in particular. "Anyway, my sister, Ruth was her name, she used to read to me and talk to me like my daddy should've. I started reading when I was just three. It got so I was reading to Ruth. She say I'm special, and I'm a do great things. I understand all that she saying, even though I'm young. She get books from her teacher and say that they for her. Her teacher happy to have a bright student. She think Ruth is bright 'cause I read the books to her, and I tell her what they say. Ruth is smart, but not like me. She bring me books on the stars and planets, books about places all over the world, and she even get a big book on medicine and the human body. One day she get a book on inventors. That there was my favorite of all. It had all kind of mechanical things in it. One day I get into my daddy's shed. He had some tools and farm equipment. I take a bunch of stuff apart and put it back together. I was only five. My daddy walk up and see me doing this, and he say I'm sure enough the Devil. He stay away from me then. He wouldn't sleep in the house with me, and after a while, he stop sleeping altogether. He stop eating, too. He gets to acting meaner than he was, and Ruth try to protect me. But she can't."

Johnny's delivery hastened and his breathing became rapid. "One day when my sister was at school and I was at home with my daddy, he get to mumbling, 'I'm gonna get you. I'm gonna get you. I'm gonna do it. I'm gonna do it.' He say that for three days 'til I guess he can't stand the sight of me no more. My daddy grab me by my throat, and he choke the life out of me. Seem like it take a long time for me to die. I saw it happen, still do. I still see his face, I smell his breath. Especially when the Gathering is here. Bet it never seemed to you that spirits can be haunted, too. But they can. Anyway, he bury my body. When my sister come home, she asked for me. At first, he lie, but she know that he done something to me. He make her scared and tell her she better not talk about nothing to nobody. My sister run off and leave. She have a life of her own, though it ain't a good one. She afraid to love 'cause she afraid to lose. But I guess you know about that, huh, Miss Ava?"

Ava shuddered, and Johnny continued his story. "My sister ain't cross over yet. She still alive, living down South, alone. Somewhere in Mississippi. She real sad. If she had some children, I could've told my story to them. I could've passed my ideas over to her kids, and they could've done all that I would have."

Johnny sat looking at Ava for what seemed to be a very long time. In fact, only a few minutes had passed. "So what you think?" he said. Ava began to cry. She cried for Johnny's life and for all the lost children whose stories had not been heard. Then she cried for her own childlessness and fell asleep.

20

the elders speak

As Charles brought his grandmother's bags in, he had so many questions for her that he wasn't sure where to start.

"I thought you lawyers were supposed to know how to talk," his grandmother teased. "I got to use the bathroom, son. You know I can't use the one on the plane, not even in first class. Too many nasty people been in there. I been holding it for some time. While I'm in the bathroom doing my business, why don't you listen to your messages and take care of your business. We'll talk when I'm done," she told him and made her way to the bathroom.

Charles just sat, still too stunned to do anything but what he was told. He walked over to the answering machine and hit the play button. He had ten new messages. The first five were all work related. By the sixth message, he heard his grandmother's voice. "Charles, you there? Course you ain't. You over there with that woman who works for you. Boy, you need to watch where you put yourself. Anyway, I had a dream about you."

Charles was thinking about how she hardly ever slept and wondered when she had time to dream.

"Don't worry about when I sleep," his grandmother's voice on the machine said. "And don't worry about how I know what I know. You been away from yourself and your people for too long, but that's another conversation. Anyway, in the dream I saw you going into that house that I told you to stay clear of. Shucks, boy, do you listen to your elders? Anyway, you stepped into something that's bigger than you. Shoot, it's bigger than me, too. By the time you hear this, I'll already be there. Oh, by the way, this is me, Grandma," the voice said just before time ran out.

The next four messages were all from Charles's secretary. The first was simple enough. "Hey, Charles, this is me. Call me when you get in." The ones that followed became more and more desperate. "Charles, I know you're out with that bitch," the last message started. "You need to call me. And oh, by the way, there was something I didn't tell you today. It was kinda hard cause we were real busy, remember?" she said sarcastically. "Anyway, you need to call me, Charles. I'm pregnant." Beep.

Charles thought of the spirit memory who held the bloody newborn and his head started spinning. Just then, his grandmother emerged from his bathroom.

"Well, son, handle your business," she said as she handed him the phone.

Charles called his secretary but dreaded the conversation. The phone rang six times and then went to voice mail. He left a sorry-sounding message. "Hey, Sandra, this is me. Got your messages. Give me a call."

His grandmother looked at him and rolled her eyes. "Some things I'm going to have to let you work out on your own. Besides," she told him, "I'm not here to deal with your love life or better yet, your sex life."

His grandmother had changed into what she called a shift—a simple housedress that looked as if she'd had it for years. The color was faded, and the fabric was worn. But it was comfortable. She had removed her wig and had tied a scarf over her long, thick, gray braids. "Well, I'm waiting," she said to Charles, who was still too shaken to do much of anything. "What happened in that house tonight? Tell me from the start."

Charles sat down as his grandmother moved behind the counter of his high-tech, stainless steel kitchen. She boiled water but removed tea from her own purse.

"I'm waiting," she said over the counter.

Charles started to tell the evening's tale. His grandmother was as good a listener as she was a talker. She interrupted him just when Charles had gotten to the point about the property and handed him the tea she had brewed. "Drink this, son," she said. It was strong but helped to calm his nerves.

Charles had to struggle to stay awake, but he did so just long enough to get up to what happened that made him run out of the house. The last thing he heard was his grandmother saying, "That's okay, son, you sleep now."

It was all the encouragement he needed. Charles did sleep, and it was a good thing, because he would need all the rest he could get.

21

acquire wisdom

In all your ways acknowledge God
and God will direct your path.

—*Proverbs 3:6*

*A*va awoke to the sound of her alarm. She took her time getting up. Daylight gave her a sense of security, but she wasn't sure just how safe she should feel. At first, it seemed as if everything had been a dream, but all doubts left when she saw something next to the foot of her sleigh bed. It was the can that the young boy had been playing with. She closed her eyes with the hope that it would disappear but knew that it wouldn't. "Alright, Ava, get up," she demanded of herself. Just as she pulled her leg out of her bed, her fear forced her to pull it back. Instead of getting out of the bed, she swung her upper body over far enough to look under it first. A wave of relief washed over her when she saw that there was nothing under her bed but her fuzzy slippers.

Ava got up and timidly checked her apartment. She took in a deep breath and realized that in spite of all that had happened, she felt amazingly energized. She showered and made herself some raspberry tea. She drank it and read her daily scriptures from Proverbs. From the time she was a child, she had made a practice of reading a chapter each day. "A chapter a day keeps the Devil away," her Sunday school teacher used to say. Today Ava felt like she needed to read the entire Bible. She finished and pulled out a pen and pad of paper. "The beginning of wisdom is to acquire wisdom, and with all your acquiring, acquire an understanding," she wrote the passage from Proverbs 4:7. "How appropriate," she said out loud. Always the good student, Ava began to outline what would be her course of action.

    I. Find out what's going on with the house

        A. Sources

            1. Schomburg Library

            2. Newspaper clippings

            3. Woman at herb store

            4. Owner of the house—maybe

            5. Any old folk still in neighborhood—unlikely

        B. Any similar occurrences in the area

            1. Neighbors

            2. Newspaper clippings

3. Historian in area
4. Newspaper morgue

II. Why me?

III. Find Ruth, Johnny's sister

Although it was the easiest to do, the last section of her outline would have to wait. She knew that wisdom and understanding must go hand in hand. Before she talked with Ruth, she would have to know what to say to her.

Freedom got up at nine A.M., which was much earlier than usual. He checked his voice mail and was rewarded with a call from Scott Baker.

"Hey, babe," Scott said, doing the Hollywood thing, "everybody was psyched to meet you. We want to move as quickly as possible on this project. Like I said yesterday, the time is right. Let's do it. Give me a call so we can set up a meeting with you and your attorney. Let's make a movie," Scott almost screamed into the phone.

Freedom was smiling and dancing as he checked the rest of his messages. They were mostly from women wondering why Freedom hadn't called and musicians who wanted him on their projects. There was one call from his mother, wondering why he hadn't visited with his cousins who were in town. " 'Cause I don't like them," he said to the message. Freedom then called his mother's voice mail and left her a message saying just that. He then took a quick shower and called his attorney. *I can run later,* he told himself. *Today I'm gonna make money.* He grabbed his phone and punched in a number.

Ava answered immediately.

"Peace. Guess who called already?" Freedom asked.

"Let me guess, your new best friend, Scott Baker?" she said.

"You got it. He wants a meeting with us right away," Freedom informed her.

"Fine," Ava said, "but you and I need to meet first. It's ten o'clock now. How about noon at my office? Then we can make the meeting with Scott at two."

"Cool," Freedom said, but he could hear from his attorney's tone that everything wasn't cool.

"Alright, I'll see you then," she said.

Sounded like she was somewhere else, Freedom thought. He rationalized her lack of interest was due to the fact that she was already researching Scott's company and what kind of deal they should make. Freedom was only partially right. She was busy doing research, and it was for him. But it had nothing to do with his film project and everything to do with what he was already calling home.

22

•◆•

precious memories

Ngozi was trying hard to remember his story. The details were beginning to fade. The tide had moved out and the memories were shallow. His memory often faded at high tide after the soul stirring had mellowed. His ability to remember his own life was starting to fade. Time was running out. But not just for him. It was running out for Freedom and the restless young men like him. He could feel it in the air. He could see it in how they were treating one another, *and he felt it in their desperation to become enslaved again. And he could hear it in their music. They were unaware of the enslavement. The economic enslavement. The ones who thought that having things made them more important. They didn't understand that they didn't own things, rather the things owned them. Ngozi knew that voluntary slavery was the greatest form of sin. It was committed against God, against nature, and against one's own self. Time was running out, but he still had the drum. He could still do something about it.*

"Yo," Freedom said as he walked into his attorney's office a little after noon. "I got this mad rhythm in my head, and I can't get it out. I think I want to open my film with it. Woo, no offense," he said, actually looking at Ava for the first time, "you look like . . . bad. You look bad. See, you need to get you some young stuff 'cause that old stuff didn't do nothing for you."

"Sit down," Ava told Freedom. "I need to talk to you, and you need to listen."

Freedom was not accustomed to being spoken to like this, but neither had he ever seen Ava in this kind of mood.

"What's wrong?" he asked as he sat down.

"It's about the house."

"Yo, Ava, I'm not trying to play your dumb games. Where's the camera?" he said, looking around.

"This is not a game," Ava said slowly.

Freedom heard the seriousness in Ava's tone, so he listened without further protest. Ava slowly, but firmly, told Freedom of the events that transpired the night before. Then she told him about what happened in her own apartment. When she was done, Freedom wasn't sure how he should respond.

"Look, Ava, I'm not good with anything too mysterious. Life is a mystery. We don't need to add no spooky stuff to it, you know what I'm saying? I'm not down with no ghosts and goblins. I believe something happened 'cause it's you telling me, but there is a logical explanation for this. And you, being the queen of logic, I know you'll find it." Ava said nothing in response to Freedom's pat explanation. "Tell you what," he said, "when we're through with Baker, we can go over there and check the house out. I'm dying to see the inside anyway."

Ava shook her head. "I'm not going back in there. I already brought something out. I'm not bringing anything else."

"Fine, then I'll go," Freedom told her. "Ava," he said reassuring her, "there is a logical explanation. We just have to find it." Freedom smiled and made a face.

When Ava didn't respond, he took another approach.

"Come on, girl, smile. I'll give you some." He raised an eyebrow and tried to look sexy. With that, Ava did more than smile; she laughed a real laugh.

"Negro, please," she told him, "give me some time to pull myself all together. Meet me back here in an hour."

Charles woke from a deep sleep. He was more refreshed than he knew he deserved to be. It was a surprise to him that he was more concerned about Sandra's call than he was by what had occurred in the house. He got out of bed and found his grandmother already awake.

"Good morning, Charles."

"Morning, Grandma," he said sheepishly.

She was cooking breakfast. "You ain't got nothing in this kitchen. That's okay, you can pick up some stuff later."

Charles prided himself on having a well-equipped kitchen. It was one of the things he dazzled women with. His culinary abilities were well admired.

"Yeah, but you ain't got nothing in here for any real cooking," his grandmother said, reading his thoughts.

"How *do* you do that?" Charles asked. His entire life, Charles had marveled at how his grandmother knew about major events before they happened. On the day his father left them, his mother had already packed his suitcase and a meal. His grandmother had told her to do so. Another time, when his grandmother was visiting, Charles had broken his arm. His mother and grandmother were in the car with the engine running, waiting to take him to the hospital, when he came screaming around the corner. "Get in," his grandmother had barked. Her "knowing" was something the family just took for granted. Now Charles wanted to know how she knew. "How *do* you do that?" he repeated.

"It's simple, Charles. I listen. Stuff is all in the air," she continued. "Most folks don't listen. Sometimes," she said, looking at him sternly, "folks who have a natural ability to hear learn to shut things out. This life is too much for most folks, so they choose to not hear."

"But it must be hard, always knowing what's on folks' minds," Charles said.

"Sometimes yes. Most times no," she told him. "If I

couldn't listen, it would be like not being able to see, hear, feel, taste, touch, all together. Getting rid of this be like getting rid of myself. You oughta try to listen more," she told him. "You'll find yourself in less trouble."

Charles ate a breakfast that beat anything he could make and got ready for work.

"You get done early," his grandmother said. "I need to get in that house."

Charles was about to leave when he stopped where he was standing. "Grandma, I'm not going back in there, and I'm not letting you go either."

"Baby," she said, "I don't know if you got the memo, 'cause most times you don't act like it, but slavery is over. Everything that's gonna happen has already started. It can't be stopped. That house is the seat of a message we need to hear, but there's something else, too. Something I'm not yet sure of how to deal with. You gonna find that no matter where you are, you will be bothered by what happened in that house. You right to be scared, but you should've been scared long before now. Pick me up at one-thirty. Now you go handle your business. It's not as bad as you think. You getting off easy this time, but the next time you act like life is a game, you gonna find out what it's like to be played with."

Charles was listening. And without her saying so, he knew that his grandmother was referring to his secretary. She smiled at him and said, "Now go on and have a Godly day."

Charles mumbled a thanks, kissed his grandmother on the cheek, and left for his office. *Thank God for this crazy woman,* he thought on the way out.

To which he heard his grandmother yell, "I heard that."

All Charles could do was smile.

Ngozi was dreaming of the homeland he couldn't get back to. He saw the beauty, the richness. He saw the shoreline. The waters had receded and the sand was within reach. Ngozi felt as if he could walk there from where he was, but he knew otherwise. He was far from home. Generations away. He looked at the lush greenery and could hear the ocean lapping onto the shore. The rippling of the water at one end and the rustling from the other. One sound danced and sang while another sloshed and pulled. It was rhythm and melody together, as it was meant to be. It was the sound that called him home. These sounds had been separated for too long. The separation hadn't just happened in this place that they called new, this America. It had spread to the shores of all of his people. He looked into the sky and saw birds that had no song. And he wept.

23

• ◆ •

Freedom's here

> We were afraid of the dead because
> we never could tell when they
> might show up again.
> —*Jamaica Kincaid*

*A*va was a whiz with research, and often lost herself in the process. Today, however, she was even more focused. Ava logged on to her computer and researched only as many entries on Scott Baker and his film company as she had time for. Most of what she found she'd expected. Scott Baker had been credited for writing, producing, and/or directing a total of fifteen movies in the past ten years. The last four had been box office hits, but not worthy of critical acclaim, while his previous works yielded eight Oscar nominations and several Golden Globe awards. One article pointed out the fact that when Scott made a box office hit and brought in lots of money, the artistic quality of the movie was low, but when he made a brilliant film, he couldn't sell any tickets. Ava knew that Freedom's involvement in a movie project would certainly draw mass appeal. Creating something that would also be brilliant would be Ava's task. Scott Baker wouldn't agree with her involvement, and for now, he didn't have to. This time her collaboration with Freedom would go way beyond legal advice.

At 1:00 Ava's assistant, Jennifer, buzzed and told her that Freedom had returned. "Freedom's here," she said, laughing. "Girl, every time I say that, I feel like it's Juneteenth or something. 'Freedom's here, people, slavery is over.' "

"Send him in," Ava said.

"You know Freedom can't wait," Jennifer said and burst into laughter. "I'm on a roll," she said and hung up. Before Ava could do the same, Freedom was standing in the doorway.

"What's up, girl?" Freedom said, grinning.

"I'd smack you for calling me girl again, but I'm too shocked to see you here on time," Ava said.

"I'm always on time," Freedom informed.

Ava rolled her eyes and laughed. "You have never been on time a day in your life," she told him.

"Oh yes I have. 'Cause when I arrive, that's the right time."

"Whatever," Ava told Freedom. "Sit down, I want you to see something," she said, handing Freedom the article she had printed out.

Freedom read it quickly. "So he does a lot of movies. I know that."

"Yes," Ava said. "But do you see the point the critic is making?" she asked.

"Yeah, that he can't do quality and box office in the same movie," Freedom told her.

"Right." Ava was smiling. "Now tell me everything that happened in that meeting, and don't leave anything out."

Freedom sucked his teeth and relayed every detail from start to finish. Ava took notes and nodded but didn't interrupt. She wrote out the questions she would ask and made marks next to the ones that would require further research. When Freedom was finished, Ava was still writing.

"Okay, professor," Freedom said, "what's up?"

Ava held up her hand and wrote a final sentence. She looked up and smiled again. "Are you ready to be larger than life?" she asked.

Freedom smiled. "Been ready," he told her.

"Then, let's go," Ava said.

"I take it you'll fill me in on the way," Freedom said.

"Maybe," she told him, grinning.

"You'll fill me in, and I'll fill you up." Freedom was reaching for the door and moving in way too close for his attorney's comfort.

"Touch me and die, little boy," Ava said playfully.

Freedom laughed. "You let me touch you, and *you* will die," he said. Freedom ran ahead to retrieve his car from the parking garage.

The work and the light mood had calmed Ava's nerves. If it hadn't been for a little boy in the lobby of her office building, she would have almost forgotten about Johnny and the events that occurred the night before. This child was not Johnny. He didn't even look like him, but he smiled and waved, and Ava smiled back.

As Ava began to walk away, the boy called to her. "Hey lady," he said, "Johnny says to tell you 'hello.' "

24

save the drama

Charles Campbell III was taking his time getting to his office. He had to prepare himself mentally for the drama that he knew would unfold. But something his grandmother said helped to ease his anxiety. Charles hadn't planned to, but found himself on Tubman Terrace in front of the house. He knew he couldn't go inside. Instead, he sat on a park bench across from the house and stared at it. It was a beautiful building, and right now, the house looked peaceful and innocent. If he hadn't seen the odd images on the staircase himself, he would never have believed such a thing was possible. Sitting here in the early morning light the house actually seemed inviting. He felt drawn to it, and he began to walk toward the house. He reached the front stairs and searched for the key he'd placed in his briefcase. He couldn't locate the key, but it didn't matter: The door slowly opened, and the feeling of warmth and comfort grew stronger. Just as he was about to step into the darkness, his cell phone startled him back to his senses. Charles grabbed his phone and before he could remember to say the word, "Hello," he could hear the familiar voice.

"Don't even think about it," his grandmother said. "Go directly to your office. Handle your business, then pick me up." She didn't wait for a response and hung up. He shook his head and almost laughed.

If he could see what his grandmother had sensed, he would have completely forgotten how to laugh.

"I almost had him," the spirit memory with the bloody newborn said. *"That old bitch stopped him, but he would have been mine."*

Ngozi moved toward the memory. He felt sorry for her, just as he had for so many in life. "Woman, you cannot exist as you did before. You want to keep a man, just as your ancestors had been kept. You must share yourself with him. You must tell him your story and nothing more."

Ngozi moved away from the memory of the woman. When he did, she laughed a wicked laugh. "I will have him," she said to the bloody bundle in her arms. "And you will finally have a father. We'll be a family. All of us. Me, you, and your daddy.

As Charles drove to his office, he tried to imagine the conversation he'd have with Sandra. He didn't have the words. He was not ready to be a father and certainly didn't want to be a husband. Sandra was very satisfying sexually but not stimulating mentally or emotionally. It suddenly dawned on him that he hadn't been these things for her either. He couldn't be a family man, not with Sandra. Instead, he'd give her a nice severance check and talk her into getting an abortion. As soon as he voiced these plans out loud to himself, his mind went back to the house and the woman with the bloody newborn. Then he thought of Vanessa. He hadn't thought of her in years. She was a one-night stand. He'd met her at a club and wanted her from the first moment he saw her. She approached him first.

"Hello, beautiful," Vanessa had said. She was tall, voluptuous, and white.

When he met her, he remembered what one of the brothers once said. "White women are wild in bed, but don't try to bring one home. Your grandma will kill you. Besides," the brother told him, "white women will give a black man whatever he wants, but a black woman will give him what he needs."

Charles enjoyed the passion of Vanessa for that one night only. She called him two months later to say that she was pregnant. She had already decided to get an abortion but thought it fair to let him know. Charles paid for it and acted like he cared.

Now his problems were closer to home. Sandra wasn't some one-night stand. She was his assistant, and while it was difficult for him to admit, he did care for her. She had been what he would call "accommodating" in every way. She was available whenever he wanted her to be and made no demands. True, she would whine about him not taking her out to business parties, but she got over it. Sandra knew what he liked and gave it to him. Still, it was not enough for Charles. He was searching for the perfect woman, even though he was nowhere near perfection himself.

Charles reached his office, took in a deep breath, and went inside. Sandra's desk was on just the other side of the door in the reception area. She wasn't there. Instead there was an envelope with his name on it. Charles pulled out the letter that read, "Charles,"

I'm sorry for the drama last night. I'm not good at this so I'll get to the point. I'm not pregnant, but I wish I were. Maybe then you'd see how much I love and need you. I'm quitting because I must. Last night I almost ended my own life. That's when I realized that I'm the problem. You never told me you loved me. You never even said that you cared about me. I pursued you because I thought you'd be the perfect husband. I was wrong. I say this not to get back at you, but for my own hearing. You only care about yourself. If I had somehow won you over, I would've been miserable. Charles, you are not loving. You are not giving. The very fact that you would watch me hurt and feel nothing, even when you are so intimately close to me, tells me that I have truly wasted my time. I don't know what has given me the strength to do this, but I quit. Send my last check to my home address. Please messenger it today, as I am leaving New York tomorrow.

Good luck in your life. You will reap what you have sown.

Sandra

Charles wanted to crush the letter and burn it. How dare she tell him who he was? "That's why I didn't take your crazy behind nowhere," he said out loud. "Clinging vine is what you are." In his heart Charles knew that Sandra was right, but his heart couldn't admit it to his head. Not just yet. For now, he would feel relief and move on as if nothing had happened. Charles wrote the check and attached a note that said, "Best of luck in the future." He called a messenger service, something he hadn't done for himself in a long time, and then he called a temp employment agency for a quick replacement. "I want an older woman," he told them. "Real old."

25

• ◆ •

the gift

> I believe in prayer. It's the
> best way we have to draw
> strength from heaven.
> —*Josephine Baker*

W hile Charles was poking around at the house on Tubman, his grandmother, Dora, had been reading the Bible. She could spiritually see that he was about to enter. She said a quick prayer before calling him. "Please Lord, let this ignorant boy listen."

Her grandmother had the "gift," as it was called, and Dora had been gifted for as long as she could remember. But when she was still a girl, she wasn't able to think of it as a gift. It was more like a curse. She would tell people things that she felt had happened and then tell them what she thought would happen. Folks didn't take kindly to her knowledge. "In a small town people are dumb enough to believe that they can do whatever they want with nobody finding out," her grandmother had said. "You can find things out without the gift in a place this small," she said of the little town outside of Savannah. "Don't you worry 'bout what folks say. God is in control. Just don't let none of their mean talk spoil you or cause you to use this gift for harm." Her grandmother was more like a mother to her than her biological one. Dora was too much for her mother to handle, or so she was told. Her grandmother taught her how to cook, sew, clean, fix almost anything. But mainly she taught her the importance of her gift and the use of herbs and other plants. "Ain't nothing spooky about who we are," she often said. "God measures out to everyone spiritual gifts. Most folks just too earthly to find 'em." Dora's grandmother raised her to feel completely normal. But others still found it hard to be around her, especially when she and her grandmother were in the same room.

Once, when Dora was a teenager, an uncle she had never met came to visit. He had been away for years and had finally returned home. Dora knew he was coming even before her grandmother. "Who's the man with the limp, Big Mama?" she asked. "He's on his way home, said he needs to be with his people. I don't think he'll be here long though 'cause he's real sickly."

Dora's grandmother began to cry. She cried all day.

That evening, her oldest boy, Sonny, drove up in a big Cadillac. "Been gone from you all for too long," he said to his mother.

"You didn't have to wait 'til you were dying" was all she said. She held her son and cried with him.

Uncle Sonny lived another three years even though his doctor had only given him three months. People said it was a combination of loving, healing, and knowing that gave him the extra time. It was time well spent.

Uncle Sonny had left when he was young to seek his fortune and to get away from what he called "pure backwardness." In truth, he feared his mother's abilities. Later on, the thing he feared became the very thing he missed most. He had made a lot of money as a car dealer, but he missed the comfort of the same backward folks that he'd tried to run from.

During his final three years, he never left his hometown. He soaked up all the love he needed and gave love and advice freely to anyone who wanted it. He and Dora had become fishing buddies. In a way he was the father she didn't know. Sonny, who's real name was Charles, had been her grandson's namesake. Dora knew that the similarities went way beyond the name. Her own brother, Charles, had also tried to run from his roots and from his true nature.

Dora put the Bible down on Charles's coffee table, where she hoped he would be forced to find it, and gathered the things she would need for her trip to the house. She had envisioned the woman with the newborn child. This was a familiar spirit. A spirit that was of the Devil. When people dabble with the occult, they often conjured these spirits. Unlike spirit memories that provide peace for the living, familiar spirits cause people to fret. Her grandson was in danger. The greatest danger for Charles, however, would come from within himself.

Dora had come close to the things inside the house before, but it hadn't been the proper time. Years before, when Charles was still a boy and Dora was on one of her annual summer visits, Dora had gone to see a friend who worked at a house on the same street. As she walked past the corner house, she sensed something unnatural. She was accustomed to spirit memories. Her grandmother had taught her all about them.

"There are no ghosts and goblins," she had said to Dora. "When a person passes over, we still hold memories of them, but because the living have not made peace with the deceased, they often create a presence in their own mind. That presence may or may not manifest itself. The spirit memory exists until the living are able to be at peace with those who are passed on."

Dora was confused by this. "So the real ghosts are the people who are alive?" she asked.

"Sort of," her grandmother explained. "The living are unresolved. In the spirit realm, you know everything and have the power to forgive. The living make a spirit memory. It's the part of what hasn't been dealt with."

"So what do I do when I see one?" Dora wondered.

"All you have to do is listen. They trying to tell their story to anybody who'll listen. You listen, and your life won't be so confused."

When Dora encountered the memories in the house years before, she knew that it was a place of gathering for many untold stories. It hadn't been her time to listen then, but the time was drawing near. There was now a purpose in the house. There was a memory that had to be heard and another that had to be dealt with. She prayed that when the time came, she would know the difference.

26

• ◆ •

getting to know you

va and Freedom arrived for the meeting. They were met by the same fanfare that Freedom had seen the day before. This time, though, there were printed proposals in front of each department head. Scott Baker was always proud of his ability to impress, but today he would go even farther. He knew a lot about Ms. Ava Vercher. She would not be won over as easily as most lawyers whose greed outweighed what was good for their client. Scott would win her and her client's confidence as well.

"So, I hear you want to make a movie using Freedom's music," Ava began.

Scott laid out his idea, as if for the first time. This time, though, he brought along visual aids in the form of charts and graphs. He had charted the ratio of blacks to whites who go to the movies, then his movies. He broke it down by regions and income. He then presented the numbers of folks who buy Freedom's music, where they lived, what video and computer equipment they had, and how many people from age eighteen to forty lived in their households. He'd done his homework. Still, Scott Baker was not ready for Ava Vercher.

"Impressive," she admitted to the room. "So where do we go from here?" she asked.

"Well, we'd like to start developing a script based on several of Freedom's signature songs. Then we hash out the 'who gets cast as who' details. Then we shoot," Scott said.

Ava smiled. "You think you can do this and still have it released in time for Oscar consideration?"

Baker, who had also been smiling, stopped. "We just want to make a good movie that depicts the life of the underclass," Baker said.

"According to whom?" Ava asked him. "Naw, brother, you want to exploit, or excuse me 'expose,'" she said, using the gesture she heard he'd used the day before. "We don't intend to participate in any further exploitation of the 'underclass.' Thanks for your time and for planting the idea. I think I know who would be willing to roll with this right away."

Ava had packed up her notes, dropped the proposal in the

trash, and was on her way out of the conference room when Scott stood up and stammered, "There's no need to be hasty."

"I'm not hasty. I'm in a hurry. We need to make our announcement before you do."

"Okay, okay," Scott said. "What's the problem with our proposal, and what do you want?"

Freedom had the good sense to be right behind Ava, and while Ava paused to give Baker another chance, Freedom was already outside of the double glass doors. Ava made a mental note to thank him for adding to the effect. She called Freedom back inside and told Baker how things would need to proceed. "We will give you a script. We will go over it with you after it's completed in, say, two weeks," she said. "Maybe three, tops. We'll give you a list of principals, and you can play with it. Freedom will of course be in control of the soundtrack and will retain a writing and producing credit. He gets foreign distribution and a cut of the film. We'll hash out dollars later, but we need to meet in a smaller room to talk about percentage points. You direct and produce the film. We write it and help cast it. By the way, Freedom will also appear in the movie. We also need to find out what you intend to do for publicity." Ava paused, but she wasn't done. Someone from the creative department was about to speak, but Scott held up his hand. "You, Mr. Scott Baker, can take it or leave it, but we intend to give you mass appeal and critical acclaim all in one movie. In other words we shall 'expose,'" she said with the gesture, "your true capability to the world. Power to the people," she added.

Scott tried to look impressed. Instead, he appeared whipped. "Can I get back to you in the morning?" he asked.

"Sure, but when you do, make sure you've read the gossip

column in the *New York Post*. We don't have time to wait. It will cost you more by tomorrow."

Ava was asking for more involvement than Scott had ever allowed. But she also knew which buttons to push.

"Fine," he said. "We'll agree to those things and work out the numbers later, but not much later," he added. "You play a little too hard for me. Do you need this in writing?" Scott asked.

"Sure, but I'll write it up and send it over for your signature," Ava told him.

"I'm glad we'll be on the same team," Scott said.

Freedom smiled, and when he did, everyone else did, too.

When the small-talk-to-make-nice was complete and Ava and Freedom had left, Scott Baker broke the silence that had fallen over the conference room. "I'm so glad they're doing the script," he said. "I have no idea what those people are saying or thinking."

Everyone laughed because they had no idea that the people they didn't understand knew them very well. Ava had learned to capitalize on that knowledge.

27

the fall

> Circumstances not only alter
> causes; they alter character.
> —*Kelly Miller*

At 1:30 Charles picked up his grandmother, who was already standing outside when he arrived. She had a large bag that smelled like all the herbs he ever heard of.

"You sure are ready huh, Grandma?" Charles asked.

"Boy, don't be sassing me. Just drive."

Charles did so, as his grandmother hummed old church songs. Every now and then she would sing songs Charles hadn't heard since he was a boy. "Come by here, Lord. Come by here. Come by here, Lord. Come by here. Somebody needs you, Lord. Come by here."

Charles loved his grandmother's singing. When she sang, she was almost a normal grandmother, old and comfortable. Charles was about to turn the corner to Tubman Terrace when his grandmother stopped singing. Her eyes became watery, and she began to cry. "So many lonely memories," she said.

"You okay, Grandma?" Charles asked.

"Yes, son, I am," she said.

Charles pulled up to the curb and was about to point out the house to his grandmother. He realized it wasn't necessary and sat silently instead. His grandmother got out of the car, lugging her bag alongside her. She slowly walked up the steps.

Things happened too quickly for Charles to take it all in. He had only turned his head for a second, and before he knew it, his grandmother, her bag, and all of its contents were laid out on the sidewalk. "Don't be pushing me" she was yelling. Charles ran toward her, cell phone in hand. He was already dialing 911. He reached his grandmother in no time and was holding her.

"You okay? What happened?" he managed.

"Boy, I sure wish you would use the gifts God gave you. Then you wouldn't have to ask so many dumb questions," she said. "Something pushed me down those stairs, and I think I broke something." She tried to move, but when she did so, she let out a loud moan. Charles had never seen his grandmother ill. He couldn't even remember her ever having a cold. Seeing her helpless made him feel helpless, too.

"Grandma, what should I do?" he asked.

His grandmother pointed to her purse, which was among

the herbs and plants that had been thrown about. "Get me my bag, boy." Charles did so, and his grandmother pulled out a plastic baggie that contained something that looked akin to marijuana.

"Grandma, what—" Before he could finish, she told him to stop thinking foolishness.

"This kills the pain, not my brain." She began to chew on it. In the distance Charles could hear an ambulance approaching. "What you go calling them for? You know I don't like no hospistals," she said, mispronouncing the word.

"You said it yourself, Grandma. Something is broken. We have to get it taken care of. You too old to just let things go."

Charles wanted to smack himself for that remark. His grandmother just laughed. The emergency attendants loaded Charles's grandmother into the vehicle, and Charles followed. The last twenty-four hours had truly been hard, but his grandmother braced herself, for she knew that the next twenty-four would be even harder.

28

yo Tayembé

We feared the heartlessness of human
beings. All of whom are born blind.
Few of whom ever learn to see.
—*Ben Okri,*
The Famished Road

Ngozi thought of the son he'd never
seen in life. Ngozi saw his son's life. He knew that he had been a wonderful son to his mother and a kind husband and father. Knowing never
made Ngozi's existence any easier. There were times when he felt what
the living would call pride, but those moments were short lived. His existence was connected to the completion of his task.

He had watched his descendants one by one, hoping that someone
would hear his story. Until now, it hadn't happened. He would soon

have the opportunity. Telling his story and passing on the drum was his reason for existing. He hoped that this boy, Freedom, would hear more than the beat. What he needed him to do was hear and tell the story. It was Freedom and all of his fathers before him that willed Ngozi to be. Ngozi's presence was the result of the unresolved issues between boys who didn't know their fathers. The boys who had no voice, no connection, no beat of their own. "Yo Tayembé. I'm calling you, Son," Ngozi chanted.

There would be one chance, and one chance only. Ngozi was running out of time. The survival of his people depended on him. The old woman, Dora, would have been able to help, but Bella, the woman with the child, had interfered. Her will, as misguided as it was, was growing stronger. Soon it would be stronger than his. He would have to act quickly. Ngozi sat down and began to play the drum. He played slowly and sweetly at first. The rhythm became stronger and more and more syncopated. The beat was now fast and furious. "Do you know who you are? Do you see what you once were? Do you feel all that you could be again?" Ngozi yelled these words over and over as he played. The playing continued. As it did, the spirit memories gathered. No stories would be told on this night. The tide was not high. The moon was not full. It wasn't time for the Gathering. Instead they would wait, like a pregnant woman who's reached full term, yet still cannot deliver. Her pains were their pains. They rocked and travailed in time with the drum rhythms, picking up the chant. "Do you know who you are? Do you see what you once were? Do you feel all that you could be again?"

This song was for the living. But somewhere in the lower part of the house, the familiar spirit that belonged to Bella sang the song for herself. "Yes, I know what I will be, what we will be again," she said to the bloody newborn. She laughed a wicked laugh and said, "Nathan, this can be our home again."

29

ye oh ye ba ba

> Don't trouble trouble til trouble troubles you.
>
> —*African American proverb*

*I*f I told you once, I told you twice. I don't want to stay here." Charles's grandmother was putting up a good fight. Once the X rays were completed and everyone knew that she had in fact broken something, her arm and a rib to be exact, there was no calming her down.

"I think it was Gilda Radner who said, 'Doctors don't know anything because they practice on the dead.'"

Charles laughed. "Grandma, how is it that you know what Gilda Radner said about doctors?" he asked.

"I can read, can't I?" His grandmother was protesting, but she knew that she would have to stay put. There was one fear that she could not shake; that was the fear of falling. At her age, which she never mentioned, falling could be the beginning of the end. Many of her friends and old schoolmates had died by the way of a fall. It was true that she had more energy and ability than folks half her age, but there was little she'd be able to do after a terrible fall. Now her fear had been realized. In a way Dora was relieved. Her worst fear hadn't been so bad. She'd mend well, the doctors had told her, but they wanted to have her stay long enough to make sure that everything was okay.

"I'm healthier than you, young man. Don't make no sense for somebody as young as you to have high blood pressure."

The doctor went pale and asked Dora how she knew about his high blood pressure.

"It's in your color," she told him.

"Well, we'd like to do some observations on you anyway," he said.

Dora did want to make sure that everything would mend properly. "I'm old, but I ain't no fool," she said. She just didn't want to be held up in a hospital or anywhere else for that matter. What she needed to do was get inside that house. She felt the pull. She also knew she'd been pushed. *Something in that place needs me,* she said to herself. *But something else don't want me near.*

"You say something, Grandma?" Charles had dozed off in the chair beside his grandmother's bed.

"Boy, I ain't talking to you, but if I had been, you would not have heard me."

"You okay, Grandma? Can I get you anything?"

"Yes," she said. "You can stay away from that house until I tell you what to do."

"That's gonna be hard to do right now," he said. "I got a call from the people who started this. I was supposed to let them in to see the place."

Charles's grandmother studied his face. To him it looked as if she were miles away, but it was only her ability to see that had left the room. Dora was trying to read the thoughts of the woman who made the call. She could see Ava clearly. Dora smiled. "Now, she would have made you into a good man, Chucky. I tried to tell you that when you were little."

"Grandma," Charles said loudly. "You okay?" His grandmother, who'd always been odd, was acting even more strange.

"They gave me something that didn't mix well with my herbs," Dora mumbled. "I think I better sleep now," she said. By the time she finished her sentence, she was already asleep.

Charles kissed his grandmother on the forehead. It was something he hadn't done in a long time. He smiled and allowed the feeling to envelop him. As he left the hospital and got to his car, he thought of Ava and his childhood desire to live between the gap in her two front teeth. His cell phone went off. "Hey," he heard from the other end.

"Hey, yourself. I was just thinking about you."

"Yeah, well," Ava said as she and Freedom sped down the highway. "This client of mine wants to go into the house, and well, I think I'm okay with it," she said. Charles didn't know what to say, but he knew what Ava was feeling. He too had felt that pull.

"Are you there now?" he asked.

"Yes, and my client is with me." Feeling great after the

meeting with Scott Baker and associates, Freedom had almost demanded that they go to the house. Before calling Charles, Ava tried again to tell Freedom what happened the night before. He only half believed her.

"Yo, you only had a bad experience 'cause you went in there with that old bourgeois Negro."

"If you think he's old, what does that make me?" Ava asked. "I told you we grew up together."

"It makes you seasoned," Freedom said slyly.

Ava was accustomed to Freedom's flirting, but lately he'd made an attempt at being charming. It made her uncomfortable and a bit giddy all at once. "Look, little boy," Ava began.

"Don't 'little boy' me," Freedom told her. "Age ain't nothing but a number. Besides, you're not that much older than I am."

Ava laughed, but she was trying to compose herself. She didn't like being hit on by clients, but she regarded Freedom as more than a client. He'd often been her sounding board. She respected his opinion and liked his aloof style. The name Freedom suited him. Whenever a deal was made with record executives, Freedom let her do her thing. He stood back, trusting her to get him whatever he needed. Most of her clients didn't have the same confidence. They all felt it necessary to tell her just how to go about doing the deal. Freedom turned to Ava who was trying to focus on the road, the house, the movie deal, and anything but Freedom.

"Look, woman," he said, "I know who you are, and I like it." Freedom didn't say another word. This was the closest he'd ever come to showing any emotion toward a woman. Ever since his childhood experience with Stacey Brown, he never allowed himself to care. It was true that he'd said whatever it took to get a woman into bed. Once or twice when he was younger, he'd even used the "L" word. He didn't go that far anymore, but he didn't need to. He knew he wasn't trying to get Ava into bed. He would have liked to, but for some reason, he was feeling like he wanted much more. His feelings had something to do with the way she handled Scott Baker. Freedom had seen Ava in action, but today she was in rare form. What moved him the most was the fact that she believed in his ability to deliver something he'd never done. Freedom was beginning to sense a lot of what he'd been missing, and he suddenly felt a tinge of loneliness. He would not admit this to anyone, but if his grandmother were still alive, he knew he wouldn't have to. Just as he was having this thought, Ava pulled up to the curb in front of the house on Tubman Terrace.

Freedom looked at the house and then back to Ava. "Yo, I know this is my home," he said to her. "After that deal you pulled today, I might even let you spend the night."

Ava laughed and so did Freedom. It was the comic relief they both needed. The mood in the car was thick enough to cut, but it was nothing compared to the mood or moods inside the house. Inside, the beginnings of a battle were just starting. Ava was still talking to Charles while Freedom was watching his house. He thought he got a glimpse of the lights he'd seen before, then he saw nothing. The whole Johnny thing that Ava told him about was messing with him. When Ava told him about the boy, he hadn't made a connection. But now, he remembered the odd kid that had run in front of his car. "Naw, now she got me tripping," he said to the air.

Ava was still talking with the attorney, but her tone had changed. "No, you're kidding. Is she okay?" she was saying. "How long before she'll be able to go home?" Ava was asking.

Freedom was only half listening to the conversation when he looked up to the second-story window. What he saw caused a scream to stir from somewhere within him. He would have let out the scream, but his grandmother had told him to be silent. There in that window the woman Freedom had called Grand, or something that looked and somehow felt like her, had raised a finger to its lips and was telling him to be still. He did as he was told. He was still nodding his head when Ava finished her call.

"You won't believe this," she was saying. She continued to talk about Charles's grandmother. It had something to do with her coming to the house and either falling down or being pushed. She said the woman didn't want them to go into the house.

"Okay, yeah," Freedom said. He was still nodding.

Ava saw that he was not paying attention to what she was saying. Instead, he was staring at the house. She looked to the window he was fixed on and saw nothing. "You okay?" she asked.

"I'm good," he responded.

"Did you hear what I said? We can't go in."

"Okay," Freedom said, "then we won't."

She wasn't sure, but Ava thought that there had been an emphasis on the word we. "I'm not playing, Freedom. You don't know what you're dealing with, and neither do I. Let's wait until we hear what happened from Charles's grandmother."

Freedom nodded his agreement, but he knew he'd do otherwise. He heard what Ava said about Charles's grandmother, but now he was listening to his own grandmother. She had never led him wrong. He missed her more than he'd realized. Now she was back. Freedom thought that he had never believed in anything spooky. He believed in God and had accepted him as his savior when he was a boy, but formal religion, especially in the black church, was too spooky for him. He didn't need any craziness in his life. He had forgotten about the childhood voices. He'd forgotten about the drum song. It was slowly coming back to him. "Ye oh Ye Ba Ba," he said to himself.

"Okay, okay," Freedom said, snapping out of what appeared to Ava to have been a trance. "I heard you, and if you believe there's something there, then I believe it." Freedom's tone had changed, and he appeared to be back to himself. But there was still something odd about his manner.

"I'd love to go get something to eat now, but we have only two weeks to knock out that script," Ava was saying. "I'm going to have to go home to work, and you should do the same. I need you to pull out the good stuff on this. None of those same tired tunes that you keep reproducing, okay?" she said.

"Yeah, I got you," Freedom was saying. Ava dropped Freedom off at her office, where they had left his car earlier. She didn't stay. She would go home and begin work on an outline that would blow Scott Baker away. Freedom was also about to begin his work. It was the work that he was here to do. The question that folks would ask for a long time afterward was why he had done it in this manner.

30

echoes

> Rap is an authentic descendant
> of a people with ancient
> African oral traditions.
> —*Mumia Abu-Jamal*

The music in the house played over and over. There was no Gathering, and therefore, there was no balance. The beat was incredible, but without the words that echoed truth, it was pure emotion. Raw passion that was poisonous. Beat with no truth was not the form that was meant to be heard. This form of music, this hollow beat, fast, furious, passionate, had been all that the descendants of the drum had connected with. Ngozi had been successful in bringing back the beat, but also had to infuse it with truth. To do that, much was required.

Some artists heard the beat that echoed from Harlem to Atlanta to California to the Midwest through swaying bodies of the young, to black Brits and over to Japan to the islands and back home to Africa. The beat was back in the rhythm of words. Words that rarely echoed truth. And when they did, it was short lived. When Tupac was moving close to truth, close to melody, close to harmony, his life was cut off. Biggie had only begun to barely see; he, too, was gone. Others were finding truth and *life*, but their music was rarely produced. The labels didn't want this new sound to survive, so without support, they either went back to the old or fell out of the scene completely. The truth was trying to come forth, but there would be a great struggle.

The beat, the rhythm, the words of hip-hop music rarely spoke the truth of the drum, but because they were chanted inside of the same syncopation, they had the ability to capture the listener in a way that had never been heard. Rap, hip hop, the beat had taken the world by storm. It was played by rebels from Nicaragua to Kosovo. The beat was copied, watered down, and sold in suburban record stores to young whites who loved being connected to something and whose parents didn't understand that connection. The music most often spoke of violence and sex in the same breath. Sometimes, but not too often, the music spoke of love and truth, but these songs were rarely popular. The righteous artists, like Amon Rashidi, The Roots, and Black Thought, who dared to use the music in this manner, were few and far between. They were not mass produced and carbon copied. It was the raw form that was duplicated and exported for the world to hear. Tonight the music from the house played loudly. Artists like Elum N Nation would awake the next day swearing they'd written their best work ever. Some of them would hear the same tune. None of them would have the ability to comprehend that this was a universal tune, a beat that belonged to all African people, a beat that would link the younger generation to the ancestors and free them from the bondage of negativity. That it was a work in progress. It was raw. "Yeah, whoever puts it on wax first" was the old saying. But first was not always best.

Freedom drove back up to the house. He, too, heard the music. He went to the side of the house as his grandmother had instructed him to do. Using a tire iron, he bent the bars to the basement window. Jimmying the lock was easy. Getting inside was easier still.

31

◆

time for all things

> Time is swiftly running out, and a new
> dialogue is indispensable. It is so long
> overdue, it is already half past midnight.
> —*John O. Killens,*
> *"The Black Psyche"*

Somewhere in a hospital, Charles's grandmother was tossing in her sleep. Ava was at home working furiously on the outline of the script idea. Charles was reading the Bible that had been left open by his grandmother. She had left markers in two places. The book of Luke, chapter 16, verses 19 to 31, was highlighted in yellow marker. It told the story of a rich man and a poor man. The poor man had a miserable life due to poverty and illness. The rich man lived in splendor, feeding his passions daily. Both died. The poor man went to heaven; the rich man went to hell. The rich man cried out for mercy and begged for the poor man to simply dip his finger in water and cool his tongue. His request was denied. He then begged that the man be able to go back and warn his brothers. But he was again denied and told that his brothers had Moses and the prophets; let them hear them. The rich man continued to plead. "But if someone from the dead could go to them, then surely they would repent," he urged. But again, he was denied. "If they do not listen to Moses and the prophets, neither will they be persuaded of someone who rises from the dead."

After reading the short passage, Charles made notes. "Why this scripture?" he wrote. Then he wrote the question that would've made his grandmother proud. "If no one comes back, who's in that house?" Charles flipped to the other marked section. It was the book of Ecclesiastes. This time the entire book had been highlighted. He read it and came to the familiar passage that had even been made into a song. "There is a season for everything, and there is time for every event under the sun. There is a season turn, turn, turn." Charles hummed the popular sixties tune. He continued to read. He read about the evils of oppression, the folly of riches, and the futility of life. The more he read, the more confused he became. Then he remembered the scripture he'd been taught as a child. "Wisdom is the principal thing, therefore, get wisdom, but in all thy getting, get an understanding."

"I wish I could understand anything this crazy woman does," he said to himself. Charles looked at the large art deco clock and saw that he'd been trying to get an understanding for almost three hours. He must have dozed off or read more than he realized. Just as he was about to call it a night, or better yet a morning, his cell phone rang. Charles had to follow the ringing to find it. It lay under the jacket he wore the day before, and he reached it just in time. "This had better be good," he said into the phone.

"Charles. Oh Charles." It was Ava, and she was crying.

"What is it? Where are you? Are you okay?" Charles rattled off a string of questions. All he knew was that Ava was in trouble. "Talk to me," he managed.

"He's . . . he's . . ." Ava stammered to find the words. "Freedom's dead."

32

the transition

> But this time, somewhere in the
> interspace between the spirit world
> and the living, I chose to stay.
> —*Ben Okri*

Charles wasn't sure who or what Ava was talking about. "What?" Charles asked in disbelief.

Ava somehow discerned this. "Freedom, the client who wanted the house, he's dead. I'm there now. I'm at the house. Please come."

Charles wasn't able to respond in words, but he was in his shoes and his car before Ava had even begun to tell him what was happening. "Ten minutes. Give me ten minutes," he told her.

Ava put down the phone and wept. Police and emergency workers were all over the place. Someone had alerted the media, and camera crews were now arriving. Onlookers had surrounded the house. Not just the white neighbors who had heard the screams, but also the black Harlemites who'd always crossed the street whenever they passed the house. An old blind man with a cane was shaking his head. "Can anything good come out of this place?" he said to no one in particular.

The officer who contacted Ava earlier walked over to her. "We need to ask you more questions. Can you come inside?"

She gathered her wits to do as she had been asked, but before she could move toward the place, she felt herself falling.

"She's fainted," one officer said to another.

"It's gonna be a long night," the other responded.

33

knowing

I just say, "Never mine, never mine, long as I
can spell G-O-D I got somebody along."
—*Alice Walker,* The Color Purple

Charles's grandmother slipped in and out of consciousness. As she'd predicted, the medicine the doctors had given her did not mix well with the herbs she had prescribed for herself. She was in a semi-private room. Dora didn't like the term "semi." In her mind, either something was or it wasn't. She didn't want anything semi or demi or halfway. Right now she wished for complete privacy. She would need it when she came to herself. Her roommate's television was on, and even though it was semi-loud, it was disturbing her sleep completely. Dora could hear a news announcer saying something about the death of Freedom. "So what else is old?" Dora asked. "Freedom been dead." She looked past the thin curtain that was supposed to provide privacy. She reached and pulled it back to get a better view of the television set. For a brief second, she thought she saw Charles escorting a woman she was sure had been little Ava, who had lived around the corner from her daughter and grandchild years before. Suddenly, a picture of the house on Tubman Terrace flashed across the television screen. Charles was in deeper than she thought. Dora tried to raise up from the bed and found that she couldn't. A searing pain ripped across her chest. Even in her foggy state of mind, Dora knew not to interfere with her healing process.

It took some effort, but she lay back and tried to think. The thinking caused a rush of pain to her head so Dora unwittingly gave up the fight and fell into an even deeper sleep. Once there, she would see more clearly. She would hear more truths—the truths that would be too profound to deal with in a conscious state. In her sleep Dora would be able to face whatever resided inside the house.

Charles had arrived just in time to help Ava up but too late to catch her. From his car he could see her falling. Her color was bad. It was the color black folks took on when their life was about to leave them. Charles knew this from the stories he'd heard his grandmother tell. He hated overhearing what he called her "ghost stories." When he was a child and trying to hear the grown folks talk, he'd sit on the steps that led to the cellar. No one saw him there, but later on he suspected that his grandmother knew and that she told these stories to frighten him. One night it almost killed him. His relatives had gathered to talk about who was seen with whom. The conversation was getting real grown when his grandmother said how she saw the spirit memory, as she called it, of a dead relative. Someone who had appeared to instruct her on how to deal with an impending danger.

"Speaking of Louise and Jim," she'd begun. "Guess who came right up to my bed last night?" The listening relatives never asked, "Who?" Dora would tell them in time. Besides, they were afraid to ask. "Jim's Uncle Gus," she said matter-of-factly. "Come right up to my bed. Didn't say a word. Just stood there with that gaping hole in his head, like it wasn't there. He was grinning like we liked each other or something. That there's a sight to see, a man with a hole in his head, just smiling at you." Dora would go on to say that she knew he was trying to tell her something and that he wouldn't leave until she figured it out. "Ain't no use me trying to sleep. I can see you ain't gonna let me," she'd told the spirit memory. She got the pad of paper and pen that she kept next to her bed and began to write as she'd done on many nights like this.

She started by writing Uncle Gus's full name and the names of his living relatives. When she finally got to the name that Uncle Gus had come about, his grin became broader, she had said. "I wrote Jim's name on that paper, and that man got to smiling like a cat." Then she would write about Jim's life and his family. Uncle Gus had indicated that trouble was brewing in Jim's love life, and it had nothing to do with his wife of twenty years. The fact that Uncle Gus, and not some other relative, had come, told Dora that if Jim didn't stop fooling around, he would end up with a big hole in his body. Charles's grandmother told the story like she was reciting a list of sale items downtown. Those who had been listening were accustomed to these stories. Charles was not. He fell down the steps onto the hard cellar floor and turned what his grandmother later called a death color. He awoke to her tapping him on the head and saying, "Come on back, boy. It ain't hardly your time. You got work to do." He remembered being sad that all she could think of was his chores. Now seeing Ava with the same near-death color, he somehow knew what she meant about having work to do. He felt that Ava, the house, and all that had recently occurred was part of that work.

When he first got to Tubman Terrace, Charles had pulled his SUV up on the curb of the park side of the street. As he got out of the car, Charles remembered to grab the business card he always left on his dashboard and then ran to where Ava had fallen. He had to cross the barricade line the police had put up between Ava and the house. Just as he reached Ava, a uniformed officer reached him.

"You can't be over here. Get back," he barked.

"She called me," Charles said while producing the business card in one smooth move. Whenever he walked, he kept one in the palm of his hand. As an upwardly mobile black man,

Charles was accustomed to being stopped by police officers. He was used to explaining his presence in the so-called good neighborhoods and had learned how to deal with the police gently. He kept a white card outside of his wallet for such occasions. Reaching for a wallet had been enough for a jury to decide that Amadou Diallo's death was not a product of racism, but accidental. It was reason enough for four police officers to shoot forty-one times. Charles, and most black men like him, lived prepared for a moment that his white peers never even thought about. His business card, which indicated that he was an attorney, along with his whitewashed manner, were usually enough to deter even the most brash officers. The card was produced so quickly that the officer looked dumbfounded.

"There's no suspect that I know of. Who are you representing?" he asked.

Ava was just coming to, and Charles moved to reach her. "She's my friend. She called," he managed.

Ava's eyes fluttered, and she could see Charles. He was talking to a police officer. "I'm here," she wanted to say but couldn't. Charles was moving away from the officer and over to her. "Help me. I saw him. He's there with the others," she said.

"What others?" Charles was asking, but she couldn't respond.

Because the media had already arrived, and because this was white row, the paramedics responded quickly. They were lifting Ava before Charles had time to figure out what he should be doing. "Step back, sir. She's in shock," the short, stocky paramedic said.

Charles did so, but in his mind he was tapping Ava on the

head and repeating the words he'd heard years before. "Come back. It's not your time. You've got work to do."

If Charles had grown up with his grandmother Dora's "knowing," he would have been able to see Freedom standing next to Ava, saying almost the same thing.

34

clarity

> Pour oh pour, that
> parting soul in song.
>
> —*Jean Toomer*

Freedom didn't really know what had happened, but he knew why it had. He knew all kinds of things now. He knew that his previous life had been almost a waste, but he thanked God for it anyway. He wished for his life back so he could relive it with the clarity he now had. He knew it would be futile to go back. He had to go forward.

Freedom waited for Ava, his friend, his love, his purpose, to come to. Once she did, he went back to the house that he would, for now, call home.

35

• ◆ •

fade to black

What key are you struggling in?

—*Fats Waller*

*A*va regained consciousness but not much clarity. "What's going on?" she wondered out loud. As soon as she saw Charles, everything came rushing back. She'd received a call she thought was a prank. It was two A.M. when the phone rang. She was already deep into writing the outline that would blow Scott Baker's mind. The phone startled her. Freedom's cell number showed up on her caller ID. She expected to hear the familiar "Peace," but instead was greeted with what had to be Freedom's best work. She waited for him to put the receiver to his mouth and start bragging. She was ready to accept all of it because the music was marvelous. It had an African feel with black soul flowing on top. It grabbed at her heart and made her want to sing and dance all at the same time. There were no lyrics, but Freedom was a master lyricist, and she knew that part would be easy for him. She marveled at how well the music fit the outline she'd been working on. Ava was listening for some time before she even thought about the conversation she should be having with Freedom. She called his name, but he did not answer. The music was blaring. She called again, expecting him to remember or even realize he'd placed a call. This kind of thing had happened several times before. Freedom had accidentally pushed the send button on his cell phone. Because Ava had been the last number he'd dialed, she became privy to more of her client's life than she cared to be. This time was probably the same thing, she reasoned. Ava figured that he was caught up in his work and had leaned on his phone, which he often kept in his front pants pocket. She was glad that he had. The music was both an inspiration and a confirmation for the outline she was preparing. It allowed her to complete her work and fall into a deep sleep. So deep that she forgot about little Johnny. So deep she even forgot about the house. Three hours later, her phone rang again. She slid from under the deep of her sleep, half expecting to hear that beautiful music. Instead, she heard the gruff voice of one of New York's finest. "Ms. Ava Vercher?" the voice commanded.

"This better be good," she replied. With athletes and musicians for clients, Ava was often awakened in the middle of the night.

"Ms. Vercher, this is Detective Don Donaldson." For a second, Ava thought this was someone's idea of a joke.

Who gave their child the same name twice? she thought. "Yeah, you got her," she said, feigning interest.

"Ma'am, there appears to have been some sort of accident, and well, we got your number from the de——." Detective Donaldson stumbled over the part of his job that always made him sweat. "Ma'am," he said, "we need you to come over to One hundred thirty-eighth and Tubman Terrace. There's been an accident, and we were instructed . . . well, we knew, to call you," he stammered.

Ava was remembering all of this now. She'd rushed to the house, hoping simply to find Freedom mildly hurt by a neighbor who mistook him for a prowler. She had even halfheartedly prepared to cuss him out for doing what she told him not to do. In her heart, though, she'd already begun to mourn. The detective wouldn't answer any of her questions on the phone, nor would he allow her to speak to Freedom. An even surer sign was the feeling she had in her gut. The peace she experienced earlier had been replaced by one of dread. When she got to the house, she was escorted inside and informed of what she already felt. Freedom was dead. She needed to cry, but couldn't. Freedom had grown from overinvolved client to friend and confidant. She'd evolved from independent attorney to a woman who could now listen to a friend. She acknowledged the growth and missed it all in the same moment. She needed solitude and sadness, but it was outweighed by her need for answers.

She ran to where the police were working, and she saw him. Detective Donaldson was trying to hold her back, but she would not be restrained. Ava made her way through the officers, medical examiners, and investigators. They were turning to her and looking as if she knew more than they did. She reached Freedom but immediately wished she hadn't. His body was at the foot of the stairs, the same stairs that had held the group whose presence had caused her to flee several nights before. Freedom's body was bent in an unnatural position. His head was angled and tilted, as if it had been pulled completely around. From his mouth had poured a pool of blood. Had it not been for the blood, Freedom would have appeared to be smiling.

Ava stood frozen, unable to think or speak. She shook her head, and her tears began to flow. They started as tiny droplets from the corners of her eyes, but soon became a flood accompanied by a wail. "No," she screamed. "No" over and over, until someone had the sense, decency, or both, to escort her outside. Television crews had arrived, and so had some of the neighbors. Ava felt as if she were in a white person's dream. With the exception of Detective Donaldson, who was black, and a Latino officer, everyone else was white. The bright lights and bright faces didn't do much to calm her emotions.

"Is there anyone we can call?" Donaldson asked. Ava immediately thought of Charles and called him. Then, she remembered, she felt dizzy. *Good*, she thought to herself, *it's nighttime, and this is a dream*. And then everything around her went blank.

When she came to, she saw that it wasn't a dream. She'd been loaded onto a stretcher, and there was something over her nose and mouth. Charles was there, but he looked strange through the plastic mouthpiece. She moved the oxygen mask and tried to get up.

"Whoa there, Nellie," a stocky woman was saying. "Down, girl. You ain't got nowhere to be just yet."

"I'm fine," Ava told her. "I need to get back to Freedom."

"He's gone, honey," the woman said. "But you know that. You just need to rest and accept it."

Charles stepped in and asked Ava to give herself a moment. "This is more than even you can handle. I'm here, and I'll do what I can to help," he said calmly.

"Don't patronize me," she said. "Freedom's dead."

Charles was still stunned and confused. It was more like a proclamation. Freedom's dead. Then everything was clear. "Your client went into the house. God no, please no," he said.

Ava's coloring, which had begun to come back, was again drained. "Freedom is at the bottom of the stairs where—" she paused, thinking of what Charles had told her about Dora, and remembering the spirit memories she and Charles had seen together. She didn't want to believe. She was an attorney, a logical woman. One of the brightest in her bright class. But these past few days had confirmed something that most old folks already knew, that there was more to life than what we could see, touch, hear, or feel. "He was where we saw them," Ava managed. "Oh, I have to call his mother," she said suddenly, realizing that she still had responsibilities to fulfill for her client.

When Freedom's grandmother died, his mother had moved back to the South. "You on your own, big man," she'd said lovingly to her son. "It's time for me to get back to my roots." Freedom's mother told Ava that he talked to her "on the regular," so getting her number would be easy. It was probably even programmed into Freedom's cell phone. Ava knew she needed to make the call quickly. The camera crew was already in full swing. Freedom tried to be low key, but was well known and popular with all of the hip-hop industry. The news would spread like fire in a field.

She counted to ten as she had done her entire life. "Don't rush into the day or nothing important," her old Uncle Brother had said. "Life will be there, but how you approach it is more important than what you approach." Ava had taken this advice seriously. Old Uncle Brother was still alive and driving, and he had to be close to one hundred years old by now. Each morning when Ava got up, she'd count to ten first. If she had to go into a big meeting or anything important, she did the ten count. She wished that she could do it now and have everything go away. She knew it wouldn't, so she would do what needed to be done.

"You need to rest a bit longer," the paramedic said.

"I've got work to do," Ava shot back. The paramedic was still trying to do her job, but Ava ignored her concern.

"Thanks for coming, Charles," she said. Charles helped Ava up.

"Thanks," she said. He led her back toward the house that had caused fear and now grief. Back to the house where their troubles had started. Back to the house that held not only answers, but Freedom, in body and spirit.

36

the more things change . . .

I believe in praising the
bridge that carries me over.
—*African American proverb*

*D*ora was asleep but working harder than she had for years. She remembered the last time she had to go to sleep to work things out like this. It had been years, and although she hadn't forgotten the incident, she no longer carried the pain. "Pain is the thing that won't let you forgive," she often told women who came to her for advice on similar matters. "Let the pain go, or you won't be able to move on in your own life," she told them.

The last time she had to work this hard was when she was still "youngish" as she called it. Her husband had been cheating on her and drinking harder than ever.

"You spooky woman," he told her. "If I had known that you were crazy, I'd a never married you. Besides, I only did it cause my daddy paid me to," he said. "We made money off a you." He laughed wickedly and told her to take her clothes off. When Dora refused, he beat her and took them off himself. He raped her, but it wasn't called that back then. Then, it was referred to as a man taking matters into his own hands. He was her husband. He could do as he pleased, and he told her so. His drinking and his beatings got worse.

Dora's grandmother had passed on. Dora didn't know as much about her abilities then. She would try to remember every detail of what her grandmother had taught her. One day it came to her to contact her grandmother in her sleep. It took her a week to make contact, but she did. Once there, her grandmother told her everything the beatings had caused her to forget. She also understood the importance of control. Dora used the wisdom to get an understanding of why her husband did what he'd been doing. Once she did, she would make him pay. Dora started reading the signs around him. She learned that her husband was the product of a loveless marriage. On the surface, things seemed fine between his parents, but when she looked closer, she could read the sadness and regret. She could also see that her husband, a grown man who was still referred to as Junior, was a disappointment to his parents. He couldn't hold down a job, even though his parents were his employers. His father's displeasure was not hard to detect, so it became apparent to Dora that she was a punching bag for a battle that went beyond her presence. When she looked closer still, she saw that the patterns of life for Junior had been generational and changed very little from father to son, and so on. Junior's mother had also been abused, but had masked her pain with fine clothes and young men from other counties.

Dora had been instructed by her grandmother to work in her sleep and to go to the root of the problem. "Ain't no need to cut down a branch and leave the tree to stand. You gotta take out the poison that's in the roots," she said. In the daytime Dora took the abuse, but at night she worked her way back to the beginning. The daily beatings had become less and less severe until one day her husband decided he could take no more of this woman or his life, and so he took his own. Dora found him and the note he left.

Dora,

Somewhere in me I love you. But I just ain't had no love for myself. My daddy would kill me for telling you this, cause he got a heap of false pride. He got his money and his ways from his daddy, and all they ever care about is finding ways to get more. My daddy's daddy was the son of a slave owner. You can tell by looking at us that we got a lot of white blood. Until I marry you, we try to keep it that way. My daddy said that by marrying you we could get things straight. I just find out that that ain't so. He tell me that your people were related to somebody one of his folks loved, and that by us coming together, things would be made right. I didn't want to marry you on account of you so black, so he paid me. Something in me really wanted to love you. Well, I guess I messed that up, too. I'm sorry for how I been treating you. I am. I told you, we tried to keep high color in the family. Sometimes our relatives marry one another to make that happen. You know what happen when folks keep marrying they own. They end up with a mess. Life ain't supposed to mix that way. I know you carrying a child, and I hope it's alright. I tried to beat it out of you. But now I want it to have some hope and that maybe our seed can have the peace I never let you have. My daddy tell me what don't work out for you in this life will have to work out in someone else's. I hope that was true 'cause not much else of the way he live is. But I guess he got it from his daddy before him. I can't hate him no more, but I can't stay neither. I'm afraid that I'm just gonna keep doing you harm. Being with you make me think about myself. I don't like what you making me see. So I'm a end it. If I don't, I know I'll end you and my seed. If I do that, my line won't have no future. Good-bye, Dora, I hope your life comes back to you the way it's supposed to.

James

Dora tried to cry but knew she couldn't. Her husband had spoken the truth about who and why he was. He had also released her from the agony that had become her life. She copied the note, packed her bags, and left her husband and his original letter for his family to deal with. Dora didn't want their anguish to be a new source of pain for herself or her child. She moved to the next county and raised her child on her own.

Dora thought of all of this in her sleep. There was a connection, she was sure. Working out life's problems usually brings you back to the circles and circumstances of the past.

She went deeper into her sleep where she could see more clearly. When she did, a young man ran up to introduce himself.

"How in the world did a cool woman like you get such a zero for a grandson? Oh, excuse me," he said, stretching forth his hand. "My name is Freedom, and I'm honored to meet you."

37

◆

Ngozi's story

> How come mister you think you
> can tell me about that old song,
> when it was born in my mouth?
> —*Mahalia Jackson*

Ngozi was remembering the life he was forced into. He saw the children he had fathered, but was not allowed to hold.

"*Please master, let me keep this one,*" *he said to no one.* "*That's when I met her. Sara was her name. She was lame, but she was beautiful. Beautiful because no one touched her. The place that had been entered by so many in other women was left alone for Sara. She had never been raped. She had been scarred by an attack of the master's wife,*" who'd flown into a rage when Sara was still a child. Her mother was being sold, and Sara tried to hold on. She refused to let go, so the woman ordered Sara to be tied to the cart that her mother was carried away in. She was dragged for miles before the driver couldn't take the wails of her mother any longer, and cut Sara loose. Her mother, who took her child for dead, grabbed the knife from the driver and plunged it into her own heart.

" 'Dumb-ass wench,' the driver said. 'Why she getting so upset over one pickaninny when she could've had plenty more?'

"Sara was left there on the road, but found later by a black man who was running errands for his master. He took her back to his plantation. The master, who was better than most but still a slave owner, protested. 'We don't need no piece of girl to have to feed.'

"The man, Jason, pleaded and said, 'The women will care for her, and she'll be able to work like everyone else.' Free labor was reason enough for the master to go along. Sara lived, but her scars were deep. She was deformed to white folks, but the black folks just saw her as one who wore her scars on the outside. When I met her, I knew she was my hope, our hope. I loved her in secret because my seed, I was told, was only to be used for certain women. Master say he need to breed strong bucks from my seed. To have come from a land where love and children were honored, and forced to produce as a bull, has brought me much shame.

"When I found Sara, I knew that I could have some small joy. She saw me looking at her and smiled. Well, it was almost a smile. That sad, crooked face told me of the pain she had been through and of the emptiness in her heart. I took her that same night. We cried together when our baby's life was conceived.

"I met her only two more times, but I watch my child grow 'til they take her away. Before they did, I teached Sara the things I learned from my mother, and Sara teach them to my daughter. It was not until I passed from that life that I could see my baby, Miella. She was bought *by a man who died the day he got her. The slaves just walk off and take little Miella with them. Her daddy and mama were free, but not for long. Miella's life was as bad as her mama Sara's. But Miella pass on the love she got to a lil' motherless child named Iona. Iona's line was troubled, but they getting to their truth. I see all of that now. I also see the reason to watch over children who don't come through you. Things pass down through more than blood.*

"So I'm passing on this drum to the one who has called me. The one who calls himself Freedom, even though he is not free.

"It was not possible for me to make the drum in life. It was not until I made my transition that I was able to do all that I was created for. The sounds that I've played have been heard by others who are also unconnected. They do not know who they are, and yet they attempt to make music that tells our story. The beat is powerful, but their message is hollow. I know this feeling of emptiness. It comes from our inability to connect to one another in spirit and in life, from past to present. Freedom will tie the present to the past. He is the son who has called for a father. We have been listening and now we have answered."

When Ngozi finished his story, he could see that many of the souls had gathered. It was not yet time for the Gathering. But Ngozi had learned long ago that the clarity he had on this side was still incomplete, and that there was only one who knew all. The souls around him began the circle of life. They created a spirit chain around him and made the music that had been lost when he did not make the drum. The music was hollow without the fullness of understanding.

At the top of the stairs stood Bella, the woman with the bloody newborn. "No," she screamed. "It's time for my story to be heard."

That's when Freedom appeared, caught up in the music. He'd walked to the top of the stairs to find where the music had come from. "Ye oh Ye Ba Ba. I hear you, Papa," he said. And then he saw her. She stood taller than him by at least six inches, or she appeared to.

"Take your child," she said, thrusting the lifeless baby into his arms. Freedom could not respond because he saw what he hadn't wanted to believe. Freedom stepped back from the woman. As he did, he saw what he thought was his grandmother.

"Hello, baby, it's your time. And I told you, when it's time, it's time," his grandmother's memory said. He was sure of it. He didn't speak this, but his grandmother nodded in agreement.

The woman with the child moved closer. "Don't you want him?" she screamed. "You told me you did." Freedom stepped back too far too quickly. He tried to grab the banister but reached out in vain. It was his time. He hit the floor below, the impact engaging the send button on his cell phone, calling Ava. The music was still being made, but now it had changed. The hollow space in his life was being filled with the life and music of Freedom's pain, joy, and confusion. He couldn't hear Ava yelling his name. He sensed it, but couldn't do anything about that just now. He was experiencing and enjoying the music. Why shouldn't he? It had cost him his life.

The others welcomed him as they had done for one another in the past. The woman with the baby was not thrilled. "You ain't nobody. I thought you was . . ." she said and walked away.

38

the reasons

We must accept finite disappointment,
but we must never lose infinite hope.
—*Dr. Martin Luther King, Jr.*

Ava walked inside the house. The fear that had gripped her earlier was replaced by sadness. "You've had a good shock and should be resting," Detective Donaldson told her.

"No, I have to contact his mother. I don't want her to find out from the news or some reporter. I have her number in my office, but I can get to her quicker if you'll let me have his cell phone," Ava said. "He keeps it, *kept* it," she corrected herself and thought of the other language adjustments that had to be made whenever a loved one passed away. "He kept it in his pocket."

"We know," Donaldson smiled. "That's how we contacted you. The phone must have fallen out of his pocket. It was on his chest when we found him. The last call he made was to you. When did you speak to him?" Donaldson asked.

"I didn't. A call came in around two, but I only heard his music. I thought he was working. Who found him?" Ava asked.

"Well," Donaldson started, "this is a little strange. One of the neighbors was coming home when he thought he'd heard music from inside. He'd seen several vehicles in front of the house in the last couple of days and thought someone had broken in and was using the place for an illegal party. He called the police and Officer Rivera found him. He's the one who noticed your number on the ID. Rivera keeps up with the music scene. He does some DJing on the side. He knew who Freedom was and knew of your reputation as well. I guess it pays to have diversity on the force, huh?"

Ava made a mental note to send a thank you letter to Rivera and a copy to his captain. "The phone," she said. "I need to use it."

"I'll do what I can, but we haven't ruled out foul play. The phone has to be dusted for prints."

Officer Rivera was sent to check the progress of the fingerprinting and came back to say that Ava could use it. Vincent Rivera was young and handsome. Too young, Ava thought, to find a dead hip-hop producer, particularly one whose career he'd followed. He escorted Ava to a side room that had probably been a parlor room back in a time when the house was grand, back before it was haunted.

"I'm sorry for your loss," the young officer said. "He had the juice, you know. He was the baddest producer who ever—" Rivera paused, feeling that he was saying too much.

"He was wonderful," Ava said.

"You have to put on these gloves," Rivera said, handing Ava a pair of latex gloves with one hand and holding the phone in his own protected palm. "They love to go over things again, and well, we just don't want to make any mistakes, especially since I told them who he is." Rivera's voice dropped to a whisper. "I'm glad I got here first. They would've treated him like he was nobody."

Ava nodded at the facts this new officer shared. Ava scrolled through Freedom's phone book list but didn't have to go far. She smiled at the fact that her number was first, and that Freedom's mother's number was right behind it. They had become more like colleagues than anything else. Making this call would be the hardest job he'd ever given her. The number had an area code that Ava didn't know. All she remembered Freedom saying was that his mom lived down South. Ava pushed the send button, and the phone was answered immediately.

"Mrs. Hudson?" Ava said slowly.

"No, she's not taking any more calls," the voice said.

"I'm her son's attorney, Ava Vercher."

"Y'all don't waste no time, now, do you, Ms. Vercher?" the woman was saying.

"What?" she said to someone in the background. "Hold on," she said to the receiver, "she'll talk to you. Sorry." The woman was curt, but trying to correct a mistake without relinquishing her right to make it.

"Hello, Ava," Freedom's mother said. "Harry told me all about you. You probably called to tell me. Some damned reporter beat you, but I thank you just the same. Truth be told," the woman said, "I had a feeling something was wrong. My boy called me last night. Told me he loved me and that he missed me. Said he was getting a place and wanted me to live with him. Ava," she said, pausing for the first time, "I knew then that I wouldn't see my baby no more." Freedom's mother could no longer contain her grief and didn't bother to try. She sobbed loudly, and Ava wept with her.

"I'm sorry," she was trying to say, but before she could finish, the woman who had answered the phone was taking the phone from her.

"It's alright girl, go on and cry. Hello," she said into the receiver, "you can call back later. We need to figure things out. We'll hold a memorial there, but the services will be down here. The reporter said he fell, but homicide wasn't ruled out. Do you know anything more?" she asked.

Ava admitted she didn't. She spared the details of the way Freedom had been found and where. She thought that all that could wait. "I'll find out all I can, and I'll contact you as soon as I do. If you want," Ava said, "I can take care of the details for the memorial on this end."

"Thank you, Miss," the woman said.

"One more thing," Ava remembered to ask. "What's your name and the name of the town I'm calling?"

"Oh, I guess that would help," she said. "This is Port Gibson, Mississippi. I'm Harry's mama's neighbor. My name is Ruth, Ruth Freeman. I'll talk to you later."

Ava was about to say something about how she'd be praying for the family, but Ruth had already hung up. As soon as she did, she remembered that she'd heard the name Ruth Freeman before. Once the thought came to her, she knew exactly where.

If she had been looking behind her, she would have seen Johnny smiling, smiling because his story had been heard, smiling because his life could be connected to something greater than his short years on earth had allowed. He was smiling because Ava and the woman who'd given birth to the new spirit called Freedom had found his sister, Ruth. Mainly, though, he smiled because his work was through.

39

can I get a witness?

*D*ora pushed farther into her sleep than she'd ever had to. The memory of Freedom was guiding her back to the house. As soon as she was inside, she felt the presence of those who had gone on and those who were still here.

Freedom came to the stairs where his body lay and looked down at himself. There was always a fascination with seeing oneself without the interference of the opinions of others.

Freedom smiled at his own form, and then stepped right over his own body.

Dora followed, as this was the path that was allowed. She saw Ava and her own grandson, but she could talk with them later. What she fought hard to get to was the center of the Gathering. There she would experience the stories of the memories that needed her to be a witness to their lives.

Freedom expressed his ideas to her, but never said a word. She heard it in the music he presented to her. "It's deep," his memory was telling her. She listened, or rather felt, the full force of the music and knew what needed to be done. She allowed her consciousness to slip back to the surface, but not to awaken. Her body still needed its rest. It was days before she would come to and find out that the doctors thought they had lost her when she told them she was never theirs to lose.

40

lessons of life

> The young get the energy;
> the old get the wisdom.
>
> —*Caroline Freeman*

Freedom's death had been ruled an accident. There were no footprints going into the house other than his, so there was no one to blame. The only other recent fingerprints that were found were Charles's on the light switch from several days earlier. The "brilliant" detectives had deduced that the music was coming from some other house and that it had been the car of the young black man that aroused the suspicion.

Ava was talking to Freedom's mother regularly to work out the details of the memorial service. The tabloid media had a field day with the loss of another one of rap music's giants. There were Web pages that pointed to conspiracy theories and speculated about whether or not Freedom was really dead.

Scott Baker announced the deal that had been made and also said that he was going on with the project. "Freedom would have wanted it this way," he surmised. He hadn't even bothered to call Ava or Freedom's mother. The labels that Freedom had worked with also cashed in on his death. An extra-added bonus to Ava's workload was the women who called Ava's office, claiming to carry Freedom's love child. Most of them were warned off easily. "When will you be available for DNA testing?" her assistant would ask. And the phone usually went dead.

The New York service was held just five days after his death. The church hall gathering looked more like the Soul Train or Grammy Awards than a memorial service. Everybody who was anybody, or who thought they were, had shown up. Freedom's family and closest friends had all avoided the New York show and had opted for the private gathering that would be held down South two days later. Charles aided Ava through the entire thing. He was connected to this situation whether he wanted to be or not. Charles, who had tried to run from his grandmother's craziness and from anything too black, had been thrust back into a life that was filled with the unknown. And to her surprise, Ava found comfort in Charles and their bond.

One day, on the way to visit Charles's grandmother in the hospital, they laughed together for the first time since the initial visit to the house. One of Freedom's songs was playing on the radio. The announcer proclaimed, "That's Brother Freedom. He's gone, but I know he's somewhere making phat music."

Shortly after the memorial service ended, Charles received a call that his grandmother had regained consciousness. During the days that had preceded, the doctors had called, saying that he'd better get there quick and that his grandmother wouldn't make it. But Dora was stronger than the doctors' predictions. Each time, her heartbeat came back stronger than ever. When the hospital call appeared on his cell ID, he braced himself for another jolt. He was jolted, but not in the way he expected.

"Where you at, boy?" Dora said into the phone. "The least you can do is come and see me after you done put me in this semi-hell of a place." Charles couldn't find the words to express the joy he felt at hearing the voice of the woman who had frightened him as a child and embarrassed him as an adult. "I know you glad I'm here, but if you listened to the voice within you, you'd of known that I wasn't going nowhere. Now get over here," she said and hung up.

Charles's and Ava's spirits were higher than they'd been since the night they met at House of Tina. "How come you stopped liking me?" he asked her during the drive.

"I never liked you," Ava said, blushing.

"You did too," Charles reminded her. Sitting next to Charles, having a normal moment allowed him to think back to easier times, times that he thought were rough but could now see in their proper perspective.

"I was a girl, and you were weird. I liked your weirdness, but I didn't want anybody to know it. Anyway, we were kids," she said and left it at that. The rest of the ride was silent and peaceful, and both felt it was good to not have to talk or listen.

Dora was sitting up in her hospital bed, drinking juice and talking to a group of young interns. "Don't let the work of this place move you from your purpose. There's a reason medicine is called an art. Be creative and remember, you are modern-day healers. Oh, here he is. Handsome, ain't he?" she said and winked at a nurse who was eyeing Charles. "Sorry honey, he's taken," she said. "You must be Ava. I've heard so much about you. Plus I sort of remember you when you were just a little girl. Gappy, they called you. You were so good for this boy. But he was strange. I don't blame you for running from him. Besides, God is in control, and look, you two done found each other again."

Neither Ava nor Charles was able to say anything. They looked at each other and laughed. Had it not been for all that had transpired, they would've thought the old woman was losing it. But now they could see just how much sense she made. "Ya'll got to get out of here. I got work to do. Go look for some other miracle lady," she said to the young interns. "The woman two doors down should be pulling out soon. Out of the coma," she added, "not life." The interns hurriedly moved to do as they were instructed. "Lord, have mercy on the young," she said. "When I get to see Jesus, I'm gonna ask why the young get the energy while the old get the wisdom. Just ain't right. By the time you know how to spend your years, you find that you done already wasted them."

Ava walked over to Dora and touched her hand. "Hello," she said simply.

"You sure are cute," Dora said to Ava. She said it as if she were letting Ava know for sure. Ava had been wondering about her looks lately. She felt that Charles had probably been attracted to more professional-looking women, whatever that meant. Sometimes she felt like she didn't have the polish that would make him ask for seconds. Charles's grandmother was grinning and laughing.

"Don't you worry none, child. When things calm down, he'll be on you like white on rice."

Ava was embarrassed and relieved at the same time.

"Now," Dora said, clearing the way for things to get serious, "y'all got work to do. I won't be able to get out of here, and don't think I haven't tried. Besides, I do my best travel at night when I sleep anyway. You all been working, but you need to set things in proper order. Pull up your chair, and get some paper out."

They had no idea they were about to receive a lesson that would beat any either had experienced in a classroom. Dora would prove to be brilliant, spiritual, and loving. She was the perfect teacher.

41

his story

Seemed to me that drumming was
the best way to get close to God.

—*Lionel Hampton*

*N*gozi was sharing what was left of
his memory self with Freedom and those who had gathered. His work
was near completion, so he could pass on what he had seen. "I only knew
joy when I was in my homeland. Joy extends beyond happiness. Happy
is what you have here. It is short lived. Joy is strength that comes from
knowing that things work together. Even when trouble comes, you can
see it as joy, for you are strong. I told you of Sara, the woman I loved
in secret. Our kind of love is the pattern many follow now. They steal

away for moments of pleasure out of fear that if this love is seen, it will be destroyed. We had to live like this. Our descendants have chosen to do so. This undercover love is more dangerous than what we lived because it is chosen. Iona, the life daughter of my child, told of her love. She was not of my blood, but she was of my spirit. She found a way to perform another kind of gathering. She wrote her story and left it for others to find. It has already begun to work its wisdom. This wisdom is seen by those who think and learn from written words, but there are those who will not hear in this manner. More of our children have been lost and enslaved to the hollow music that gives no strength; it gives no joy. Freedom's music will find its way to them, and they will listen. Still others will need more, so your stories must be told. They will find a vessel in one who listens and passes on our truths. Balance, the harmony, the beat, the words will come together. The music must tell them the truth. To love, forgive, and never forget. Tell them to search for peace and to honor wisdom. They must allow the elders to be a part of their lives. This has been missing. They must value the gifts they have been given and never use them for destruction. Speak truth to power. Come back to God and yearn for all that is good. When they do, we will have redemption.

Ngozi disappeared, but to those who had looked to him and listened to his wisdom, he could never really be apart from them. They understood the principle behind the scientific parable that says matter is neither created nor destroyed; it just changes its form. Ngozi, the blessing, was with them and everyone else.

Bella, the familiar spirit that held on to the dead baby heard all of this and began to cry. Ngozi had told her that she loved in death the same way she had in life. What she called love was not. Her spirit was possessive and unforgiving. Love and unforgiveness could not dwell in the same place.

She could not let go of the things that had caused her pain. Because of this, she could only inflict that pain on others. Freedom was not the one she searched for, but he had been similar to the man she longed to find. She could tell. He had been the kind of man who promised love just to get his physical needs met. It didn't matter to him that he left behind a broken spirit and sometimes, as it was in her case, the broken body of a child. They took what they wanted and left. But what she did not know was that by failing to forgive the man who caused her this pain, she had become like him.

Ngozi was right about this, but it didn't matter now. He was gone. Freedom's presence was powerful, but it was new. She had been this way for many years. She decided that she would control him, and in doing so, she would stop the work that needed to be done.

42

◆

Sister Space

> Take off your shoes,
> you're on holy ground.
> *—Exodus 3:5*

*A*va and Charles had been given their instructions. Dora had rambled on for some time, demanding that they take notes. At first, nothing made any sense, but as the hours progressed, so did their clarity. The first task was to get to Sister Space Books. There, Ava was to talk with the two owners. Ava had been there once before but found Valentine, the taller of the two, to be the opposite of her name. Miss Althea was nicer, but only by a little bit. This second visit enabled Ava to see she had been wrong. This time, Ava watched the way the owners directed customers to books they didn't know existed.

"You don't want that book, girl. This is what you need. Just buy it, and read it," Valentine told an indecisive customer. Now she knew why Miss Dora wanted her to see Sister Space.

"Those two have clarity and a spiritual base," she had said. "Don't let them fool you. They're softies, but in their business, they can't afford to show it. They're not just about the business of selling books," Dora had replied to an unspoken query. "They're about the business of teaching women how to heal and then serve one another. They look like booksellers, but they are warriors, child. Don't be fooled."

When she approached Valentine and Althea, Ava bowed her head slightly in deference. "Good afternoon," she said. "Miss Dora sent me." A young assistant was called to take over the counter, and Ava was escorted to a room in the back. The room was set up like a large classroom. Author readings and instructional courses, among other events, were held there. At the front of the room an altar had been made. It held objects of the earth and objects of art. The air was filled with an aroma that was sweet like an oil. Ava couldn't put her finger on the scent. At first she thought it was frankincense. Then, she thought she smelled sage. The aroma shifted again and became myrrh and patchouli. "What is that wonderful smell?" she asked.

"Little bit of this, little bit of that," the women said, laughing.

"Miss Dora sent me here and said that you would have something for me. That you would know what to do." Ava felt like a schoolgirl sent to run errands for some of the older neighbors. Because she'd been bright and good with math as a child, she was often called on to play the numbers for them. Being in the bookstore had brought this memory back.

The women were studying her face, looking to see if what she was saying was true. Once they determined that it was, Valentine got up and went into a room that was behind the one she now sat in.

No telling what's back there, Ava thought to herself.

Valentine returned with what appeared to be a manuscript. "This is what you need, this and a prayer," Althea said. They stood and gathered hands and prayed. "Lord, make us true and thankful. Keep us mindful and focused on your perfect will. Surround us with the love that protects from all danger. Amen."

"We got this from another one of our sisters. Perhaps you've heard of her? Her name," Valentine said, "is Cosina Brown." Ava looked down and saw that what Valentine had retrieved was in fact a manuscript. It was the original manuscript of *Redemption Song,* the book that had been like a *Celestine Prophecy* or *Alchemist* for black folks. Ava had read *Redemption Song* and enjoyed the way it weaved the story of love between an enslaved man and woman with the love of their modern-day descendants. It was a fun read and had become a popular and almost cult-like phenomenon. Valentine stared into Ava's eyes and proclaimed, "This wasn't just a fun read, Missy. Every bit of it was true. Now that you've witnessed the Gathering, you should know that."

"I need to read it again, don't I?" she asked.

"Whoo, girl, you brilliant. You should be an attorney or something," Valentine teased. This time, though, she smiled, and before Ava could return the gesture, she was being led out of the store. "Time to do your work, and we got ours to do. We can't hang with you all day, no matter how important you are, huh, Althea?" Valentine said.

"That's right. Don't lose that manuscript. Don't worry, sister. Dora said it will be fine," Althea told her.

Ava didn't know what they were talking about, but she found herself believing them.

43

testing the spirits

> Be concerned, but don't worry.
>
> —*Pastor Ralph Buchanan*

Charles's task had not been as easy as the one Ava was sent to perform. He had to go back into the house. He'd been sent there to leave something. Now he was praying that nothing came out with him. Dora instructed him to set up candles and burn sage in the northern most corner of each room. He was to pray and read a passage of scripture before he left. He had no idea that the candles and sage burning were for him. Dora would tell him this later. For now, she'd allow him to think that he could actually ward a spirit off. The sage was burned to give him comfort. The candles were lit to represent the illumination of his own light. It was the scripture, the word, that would do more than any other ritual could.

Charles had been put at ease. On his way out, he opened the Bible to 1 John 4: "Beloved, do not believe every spirit, but test the spirits to see whether they are from God because many false prophets have gone out into this world. By this, you know the Spirit of God. Every spirit that confesses that Jesus Christ had come in the flesh is from God. And every spirit that does not confess Jesus is not from God. And this is the spirit of the anti-Christ of which you have heard is coming and now is already in the world. You are from God, little children, and have overcome them because greater is he who is in you, than he who is in the world."

Charles had read the scripture before coming here. His New Age worldview didn't want to accept a distinction that was so narrow, one that only spoke of Jesus Christ. But by his third reading, he could see that the thing that needed to be tested was spirit. If the *spirit* rejected Christ, it was not from God. He saw the importance in this clarification, since the spirit realm held a much broader perspective on what was real. He felt the power he received from this reading and wanted to challenge the inhabitants of the house right then. But he'd already been instructed to read and then leave. He did as he was told. Dora was glad for this. If Charles had seen what he had stirred, he would have been glad, too.

44

going home

> Life is all in the play.
> How you play is how you stay.
> —*Freedom*

With the assignments completed, Charles and Ava were free to travel to Port Gibson, Mississippi, for Freedom's home-going service. They were amazed to see the beautiful woman who was his mother. Earlene was fifty-five, she said, but could have easily passed for thirty. She had the same intense gaze that Ava thought Freedom had created on his own. She now saw the source of the look.

"Thanks for everything," she told Ava. "Come on in and meet the rest of your family." She was holding Ava's arm on one side and Charles's hand on the other.

Once inside and introductions were made, Ava and Charles settled into the flow of the conversations.

Relatives shared stories of Freedom's childhood and transition into manhood. "That boy knew how to make an entrance," they said, laughing after hearing the story of his birth.

His mother was laughing, too. Her laughter slowed, and as it did, she moved closer to Ava. "Alright, child, we know the story of how he got here, and we talked about what he did while he was here. You the witness to his passing. You gotta tell us what you know." Before Ava could protest, Earlene stared at her with the Freedom intensity and said, "This time, don't leave nothing out."

Ava thought over all she knew and realized the ritual she was seeing was similar to what had gone on in the house. It was a gathering of the living. A ritual that was performed to enable the life of the deceased to be remembered. This link between the living and the dead played a crucial role in the transition. It was why black folks spoke of the dead as if they were still alive. She looked into the faces of those who had gathered. They were folks who would not have been invited into the New York service. They would not have been thought to be important enough. Only weeks before, she herself would not have been able to see just how important they were. Now she knew that these simple country folks were wiser and lived better than she herself did. They understood that prosperity was not in material wealth and could not be measured. For them, prosperity was peace.

Ava began her story. "When Freedom, I mean Harry—"

"That's alright, girl, call him by the name you knew."

Ava smiled. "When Freedom wanted something, there was nothing that could keep him from getting it."

"Um-hmm, that there's the truth," they proclaimed. "That boy set his feet to something and did it."

"Sure did. Remember the time he wanted to catch a fish, but couldn't?" a relative said. Everyone started laughing.

"Ava," someone else said, "that boy had been out all day. When he couldn't catch nothing, he jumped into the river and tried to find a fish and bring him back in." The room rocked with laughter.

The clamor died down, allowing Ava to get back to the tale. She told the whole truth, but not in the order that it happened. She waited to the end to tell the story of Johnny. When she did so, she turned to Ruth and said, "Miss Ruth, your brother Johnny is free now, too. He wanted me to let you know." Ruth, who hadn't shared her childhood with anyone in the room, was crying. She stood up, trying to leave. Earlene went to her and held her.

"Go on, child, tell the whole thing."

She told them about Johnny, the fifty-year-old spirit memory that appeared to her as a body of the young child. "He was there to help guide us and bring me to you. I see now how connected we all are, how my family and yours come together now to complete the unfulfilled longing of the ancestors. I've been hearing things that only touch the surface of where we need to be. I'm just grateful to be a part of it."

To Charles's surprise, not one person in that room found

this tale to be unbelievable. It was true because Ava said it was. But also because they all had their encounters with memories of others. These memories were carried with us. Sometimes they haunted us. This Ava learned due to our inability to forgive and let go. Memories, she learned from Miss Dora, are stored in our minds. Spirit memories are a manifestation of what we have stored. When we have unresolved issues with the dead, we cause them to appear as spirits. Ava had been amazed when she first learned this. She had always heard that the spirit had the unresolved issues.

Miss Dora had said, "If you in the spirit realm, why couldn't you know how to forgive the living? You're either in a much better place or wishing you were," she said, referring to heaven and hell. It all made sense now. "Ain't spooky at all," she said. Now Ava could see that death was a normal part of life. She was able to have peace.

The service was not long, but it was eventful. Others, who had not been at the house but were fans from neighboring cities or just folks who like to show respect, had crowded into the church along with the family Ava had met before. Some of them cried openly. Earlene was fanning herself and looking sternly at those who she'd later proclaim were trying to "create drama." "Those folks create drama just so they can star in it," she said. The minister's sermon was short but powerful, professing the love and comfort of Christ to all who were connected.

As they drove to the burial site, Ava marveled at the way passing cars all pulled over in respect for the family. "This doesn't happen in New York," she told those she shared a ride with.

"That's why we live here," someone responded.

After the burial, a woman sang a gospel rendition of one of Freedom's songs.

> Life is all in the play.
> How you play is how you stay.
> Stay long enough you leave enough to be enough.

In Freedom's version, the meaning was not this clear. Ava cried for her own loss and smiled for the love she had for Freedom.

Ava and Charles stayed an extra day and took time to relax. This was another one of Dora's instructions. On the day they were leaving, they drove to Freedom's mother's house to say "thanks" and to receive huge packages of food. They were surprised to see Ruth and Earlene's bags waiting for them on the porch. They were smiling when Ava knocked on the screen door.

"Hey, ya'll ready?" Ruth asked.

"Ready?" Charles said, somewhat baffled.

"Yeah, we going with you. There's a presence in that house that must be confronted. You think we're gonna let you do it alone? You're crazy. Besides," Ruth said, "my brother was there for a reason. I have not told anyone about his life. I was wrong. By telling the story of him and all he knew, I could have given him rest. He wanted to pass on his memory to others. Instead, I caused all the energy to remain locked up. Let's go," she said.

Ava and Charles would not argue with these two. They reached the airport to find that the women had already purchased their own tickets.

"When did you have time to do that?" Charles asked. "We

did it online," Earlene said, laughing. "Y'all think New York is the only place where they got computers?"

Charles laughed. "Touché," he said.

"Oh Lord, here go black people trying to be French," Earlene quipped.

45

the voice within

> Swing low, sweet chariot,
> Coming for to carry me home.
> —*Negro spiritual*

*T*onight my story will be told," said *Bella, the familiar spirit of the woman with the dead baby. "And when it is, your father will come back, and he will love us. And if he doesn't, he will die a death more horrible than my own."*

The group arrived in New York at eight o'clock in the evening. They went right to the hospital, only to find that Dora had checked herself out. Charles called his house and got no answer. He called his cousin, Goober, at his grandmother's house and was told to go handle his business. "You should listen to the voice within you, and you would know not to worry," Goober said and hung up.

In his spirit Charles knew where his grandmother was. He didn't want to hear. He had no desire to listen to the voice from within. It was telling him that Dora had fought the good fight.

46

●◆●

when purpose collides
with destiny

They drove to the house in silence. Charles was holding back tears. Ava held his hand the entire ride. She sensed something was wrong, too, so she drove. When they reached the house at 138th Street, Ava looked to him and said, "Everything will be okay."

"I know that," Charles said. "I just don't like it right now."

They used the key to enter and found that the house was amazingly still. The unlit candles and sage were in all of the corners where Charles had left them, and the four went around and lit them. "This lighting is better," Charles said. He was taking charge in a way he hadn't been accustomed. He climbed the stairs slowly. He had not called out to his grandmother and knew there was no need to. She had made her transition. Before, he would have said she was dead. Now he knew better. He walked to the top of the landing and found his grandmother's body. She was lying peacefully on her side. From behind, she looked like she had been sleeping. Charles walked around to face her. He wanted to thank the body that had been his grandmother. He knelt down to pray. He looked into the face of the corpse. What he saw was the embodiment of sheer horror. His grandmother's face was contorted into an expression she had never shown in life. It was that of one who'd been terrified.

Charles didn't have time to react to what he saw. Someone was caressing and kissing the back of his neck. He knew immediately that the touch was not human. He spun around and saw what Freedom and his grandmother had seen. It was the woman with the dead child. This time, though, she was not alone. Beside her and around her were a host of other lost souls. Souls whose death brought no more peace than their lives had. How they died was how they remained: bloody and hideous.

Charles couldn't scream, but there was a pull of energy in the house that caused Ava, Ruth, and Earlene to leave the rooms they were in and run to Charles. They tried to reach him but found that they couldn't. They were tossed back down the stairs as if they were nothing.

"Leave," the woman hissed. "He belongs to me." Ruth, the sister of one who had resided here, stood to correct her own errors. "Tell your story," Ruth commanded the woman. "We have come to hear you." Gathering now on the lower landing were those who accepted God's truth and knew that God was in control. These memories were the witness to Christ's resurrection. They were many. Among them was Freedom, and now Dora. Both were smiling. Ruth did her best to ignore them. This was a battle for the living. The years of grief had taught her this. "Tell your story," she commanded again.

The woman smiled, "Alright, and then he comes with me. I was always beautiful," she began, "but when I started singing, I was something else. My folks raised me to know that I was better than all the other black girls. I was, too. I could have anybody in my town if I wanted, but none of them were good enough. My daddy told me so. He loved me and showed me the secret love that a daddy has for his daughter. He said that I could do things for him that my momma couldn't. Anyway, when my daddy died, wasn't no more reason to stay in that deadbeat town. I left for New York 'cause I could sing. I got a job right away. With my looks and my voice and my daddy's money—he had left me plenty—I could do what most black women never dreamed of. I hired my own band 'cause I wanted them to complement me, and not me complement them. I got jobs at all the best places. That's when I met you, Nathan." She was saying this to Charles. "You were one of the biggest racketeers in New York."

She let out a cackled sound that was supposed to be laughter. "He owned a big ol' nightclub. Had something to do with that racket money. I sang there lots of times. White folks came from all over to hear the Black Angel. That's what they called me. Folks only talk about Billie Holiday, but I gave her a run for her money. I'm a tell you that. Anyway, Nathan and me started looking at each other, and he started whispering to me between sets. Before I knew it, we were doing that thing. Nathan was good to me. Told me I deserved the best. I loved him more than any man I know. Even my daddy, 'cause Nathan, you can see, is *white, and wasn't too many white men who would show their black woman off back then."*

Ava was as confused as the others were, but she hadn't expected this night to make any sense.

"We did our thing every night, right there in the back of the club. One thing led to the next, and I got pregnant. I was so happy. I knew my man would be happy, too. I told him, and he punched me so hard, he broke my face. I said, 'What's wrong, Daddy? Ain't you happy? We can be a family now.'

"'Black whore,' he said. Told me I was stupid for ever thinking he would want me. He dragged me out back and put me in a car. His driver came out and took me to some man who said he was a doctor. The man was crazy. He feel me up and tell me to take off my clothes. I didn't know what he was gonna do, but I thought that this was the doctor who was gonna make sure my baby was alright. I figure Nathan had a change of heart. He didn't, not until now, huh, Daddy?" she said to Charles.

"That man who say he was a doctor still rubbing my legs. Then he put a metal thing inside me. I'm screaming, but he just smiling. He say when he done, maybe we can go someplace. I hear something inside me snap, and he must a hear it, too. All he saying is 'Uh-oh. You farther along than I thought.'

"My baby came sliding out of me, but he don't say nothing. He don't say nothing. I felt the blood and life running out of me. I see that doctor calling Nathan. He tell him to come and get me, that I'm dying.

"But Nathan say, 'That black whore's your problem, not mine. You the doctor.' None of that matter 'cause I'm already dead. But I knew if I waited, you would come around. Took you a long time, but you came back to me, Nathan.

"Here," she said to Charles, "come hold your baby boy."

For a second, no one spoke. Charles was trying to move away from her just as Freedom had. He had managed to stand, but the lost souls had created a circle around him. He looked down to his grandmother's memory and realized that she was letting him listen to the voice within. In his mind he played back all that had occurred. He remembered the scripture he'd read and the confusion he felt after reading Ecclesiastes. Now he saw its importance. In the end, the only thing that mattered in life was that we honored God in all that we did. In that we were to also honor those who had gone before us. "You are a memory of something lost, nothing more," he said to the dead woman.

As he did, the woman turned as if to walk away, then suddenly she raised the bloody thing that had been her child and struck down hard. "Take your child," she was screaming. Ava ran to help, but again was thrown back. Freedom stepped forward.

"Yo," he said, "I was made in the night, but it wasn't last night." He opened his mouth and released a sound that was beautiful and powerful. It was the music he'd been sent to make. It was righteousness rolled into sound. The beat and the melody had merged. For Freedom, purpose had collided with destiny. He had taken all that Ngozi had given him and infused it with the memory of his only life. The fathers had now joined with the sons, and the path of those lives was completed. The woman turned and watched as those who had joined her now left her side. They moved toward the music.

Freedom's mother, Earlene, cried for only the second time since Freedom's death. He looked at her, and she knew that all was well with his soul. His life had been a mess, but he had accepted the Belief as a child. He walked in that Belief even when his actions did not reflect it. Now she knew that nothing we did could win or lose redemption because redemption has been won for us.

The spirit woman was on her own, and now it was Ava's turn. "You have a choice," she said, approaching the memory. "You can choose to forgive or continue to suffer."

"I can't," she said.

"Learn to love, strive to love 'cause we ain't got time for nothing else." Ava recited the line she read in Redemption Song, the line that Valentine and Althea knew would be empowering. "I love you," Ava said to the woman. "And I love you," she admitted to Charles.

He was unconscious but in a state where he could perceive what was occurring. He wanted to tell Ava that he deeply received her love, her forgiveness. He needed forgiveness for all the hurt he had caused to others. But he wanted peace from Ava.

"You're already forgiven," Ava said.

Bella, the spirit woman, looked at Ava. She was tired. She had held on to her death long enough. She had also been responsible for the deaths of others. She treated every man who came to the house on Tubman Terrace as if he were Nathan. Only when they had finally crossed over could she see them for who they really were. Now it was time for Bella to settle into her spirit and be her true self. It was time to forgive. "Time to be free," Bella said. "I forgive you," she said to Charles. "Sleep, baby," she said to her child. "Go on and sleep. Mama needs to rest." When she did, she was released and so were the others.

Freedom left, but he left behind the righteous music. Ava was physically tired, but her spirit was revived. She had to deal with the matter of Dora's death and explain their presence there, so she called the police.

By the time the police arrived, Charles had come to. They decided to report that his grandmother had come back to the house because she was delirious and looking for Freedom. This was a tale that he would have been whipped for, but Charles knew the police would buy this and not what really happened.

When the paramedics lifted Dora's body and placed it on the stretcher, a tape recorder fell from her hands. They all looked at each other, wondering what part of the evening's truth had been recorded. An *officer rewound and played the tape. The only thing on it was the phat, righteous music that Freedom had made.*

"Your grandma sure liked good music," the officer said, handing Charles the machine.

"Yeah, she sure did. She surely did."

epilogue

*A*va and Charles were now locked in purpose. They would work together and grow into love. They proceeded to do with this music what had been done with *Redemption Song*. The tape was released as Freedom's last work. But after Earlene went through Freedom's things, she found a collection that would put Prince's vault collection to shame. The music opened up a new wave of opportunity in the recording industry. Labels now looked for artists who could duplicate the sound.

Ava was about to strike up a deal with Scott Baker to make a movie, but she found out she had the backing to do it independently. With Earlene as a backer, she had all the finances she needed. Some of his friends from the hip-hop world worked for less than scale, while others donated their time and talent free of charge. The movie was the story of Freedom's life, his music, and his transition. Charles and Ava told the whole story, including the occurrences at Tubman Terrace. It was received with rave reviews. One critic called it the perfect marriage of real life and fiction. Someone else called it a ghost story with a righteous beat. The film broke box office records and won numerous awards, including several Oscars.

Ruth and Earlene funded other independent projects under the name of "Freedom Lives Productions." Their offices were, of course, in the house on Tubman Terrace.

acknowledgments

There is a feeling of reward that one gets when writing acknowledgments. It represents many things. It is a sign of the completion of a project and more importantly, it reminds one that without the help and support of others the project could not have been realized. That is the reasoning behind my dedication. It is given to those whose purpose is found in supporting others. The list of names of supportive people would be longer than this book. The majority of people who actually get things done, who are the real movers and shakers, the proverbial wind-beneath-our-wings, hardly ever see their names. I would like to acknowledge some of them now.

*T*he concept of the book came to me when a longtime friend and hip hop producer, True Master, took me to a brownstone he wanted to buy. True is a night creature and when we got to the house there was no electricity, and the place was downright spooky. Additionally, at that hour, with just a small flashlight to guide us, the floor didn't look safe. Still, I could tell as he showed me around that he was excited about the prospect of moving in. I, however, was looking for something to jump out of a corner. That's when I got the idea for this book. I am grateful to True Master for sharing with me the haunting experience of his now wonderful home (not to mention the gift of his incredible music).

Shortly after I began writing, my brilliant editor Janet Hill introduced me to Harry Davis, an insightful, and creative young filmmaker who has a presence that won't go away. He embodies the spirit of Harry/Freedom in his need to create work that is truly reflective of our struggle. Thanks, Harry.

In *Redemption Song*, we met Miss Cozy, who was based on Emma Rogers of Black Images in Dallas, Texas. Emma has a partner, Ashira Tashany, who also has spoken into my life. Thank you, Emma and Ashira for your guidance.

*D*uring the book tour for *Redemption Song*, I came into contact with other wonderful booksellers. These folks are gems to their community and to the world of literature. Fay and Cassandra of Sister Space in Washington, D.C., are included in this book. Thanks for the healing. The place is deep. Blanche Richardson of Marcus Books in Oakland is a real descendant of Marcus Garvey. There are many others I will introduce in my next book.

*T*hanks also to publicist Gail Brussell, interior designer Dana Treglia; editor-in-chief Bill Thomas (thanks for getting it); my agent and editor (to whom I dedicate this book); and to Melissa Rivera's husband, Dino Martínez, who helps us with this movement. My mother, Beatrice, and my children, William, Jabril, and Fatima who are amazingly supportive of all that I try to accomplish. My sisters who put up with my ramblings: Ava Beard; Christine Berry, Tanya Berry, Dr. Bernita Berry, Ollie Calvin, Dawn Cone, Marcia Dyson, Starla Lewis, Dr. Barbara King, Johnnie Mae Chandler, Callie Spillman, Suzanne Burnell, Lavetta Buchanan, Tia Thompson, Cheryl Hardwood, Jennifer Porter, Bethany Pickens, Vikki Hardy, Dora Taylor, Dalonda Groomer, Novia Taylor, Terry Davis, Ruth Watson, Kalada Salaam, and Rocki Rockingham. My brothers Kevin and Brent Berry, Mumia Abu-Jamal (you will be free), Kevin "what are you doing" Sanders, Wantaregh, Brother Haki Salaam, Kasimu Harley, Terry Evenson (wouldn't be here without you), Jim Keinz, Winston Scully, Michael Asbury, Stan Spillman, Vince Stokes, Will Downing, my spiritual teacher and pastor, the Pastor Ralph Buchanan.

*T*hanks also to the readers who e-mail, call, write and stop me in the airport, encouraging me to keep writing . . . don't stop telling me.

*T*hanks to everyone who reads. The brothers and sisters behind bars who, through certain circumstances, are still finding their purpose . . . believe in yourselves and don't lose hope. It's not too late. To the ancestors who are still fighting for our freedom. By the way, like Black Images in Dallas, Sister Space Books actually exists in D.C. Go, call, or e-mail. But be ready to hear the truth. Much Peace. Much Grace.

*H*ere's a special preview of *Jim and Louella's Homemade Heart-Fix Remedy,* a sizzling, smart, and utterly engaging novel about sex, love, folklore, and family history from Bertice Berry.

A Doubleday hardcover on sale in August 2002.

CHAPTER ONE

Discovery

"Possibilities are like promises:
they only work if you work them."

*I*t all started when Jim couldn't get it up. I guess I should find another way to say it, but we just country folks, so that's how we put it. That was two months ago, and he been 'fraid to try ever since. Anyway, we'd been married for twenty-six years and have had more than our share of it in the love department. We youngish still, me somewhere at the end of my fifties and Jim starting in his sixties. We got a lot of love left. I told Jim just that, but it didn't help none. In all our years of marriage and the three before, I've never seen him so upset. Jim has lots of pride and he don't like the idea of not being able to do his business, so I stopped trying to talk sense into him and did the next best thing.

Now, I've learned years before not to take stock in none of those women's magazines. Their sex tips usually include food or Saran Wrap, and Jim didn't like nothing too messy. He say the only thing he wants wet is me. Anyway, whenever things were tough with me and Jim, I pray that God will give me strength, make me humble, and show me where I'm wrong. Then, I talk to the ancestors. I talk to them like they still alive too, but I do it in my sleep and they always know the answers. This time I call on the women: my mama, Aunt T, and Grandma Sadie. They a hoot.

Mama say, "Hey, girl, don't say a word. We know just why we here."

"Uh-huh," Aunt T say. "Jim can't do the do."

Grandma Sadie tell her to hush. She say, "Your man weren't too good *no* time." She say it's better to have a man who have it but lose it all the way once, than to have one who never lose it, but only halfway does it the rest of the time.

Now, I laugh. Grandma Sadie tell me that our problem is that Jim and me done got way too comfortable with each other. She notice we hit it every Wednesday and sometimes on Sunday (depending on how good my fried chicken is). Until then, I didn't know about that connection, but I vow to take more time with Sunday dinner from that point on.

Mama say, "Girl, you need to spice things up a bit. Fix your hair and put on a little makeup."

Mama know that I ain't into nothing too fancy, but I remind her anyway. Aunt T say I need to learn some other positions. She say I got the wife and the mother part down pat, but I need to be a bit more whorish in the bed-room.

Grandma Sadie say, "Hush up, good loving ain't in no makeup, and it certainly ain't in no slutty ways. If the man want a whore, he'd pay one."

Grandma Sadie say the loving in the bedroom is in all the things you do before you get there. She also say me and Jim are real good to each other, better than most, but we need to find one another all over again.

I ask her what she mean, and she say, "Girl, when the last time you rubbed that man's behind?" Before I can act shocked or tell her "never," she say, "Uh-huh, that's what I'm talking about. Jim knows what he got, and he thinks he knows how he likes it. What makes a man hot is making his woman hot. He thinks he knows just what to touch and how to touch it. In all the years you've been married and all the time you were sneaking around before, Jim ain't had to figure out too much. He made you happy in bed because he made you happy in life, but girl, there's a lot more you should be doing."

At that point I want to ask what, but I hear Jim getting up, so I do too. I roll over and see Jim lying on his stomach. I can tell that he's feeling badly because it's Wednesday, and in the morning he's usually feeling like he want it. Most times, but not always, he gets it too. Usually, I wait for him to come to me, but this time I go to him. I rub Jim's behind slow and soft at first. I hear him moaning real low.

"Mmm baby, that feels good," he say.

I rub it some more, and he turn over. And I see what I

hadn't seen in a long time. Mr. Jim, that's what I call him, is standing at full attention. Jim so excited he can't wait to say hello to Miss Lou. That's what he call me down there, on account of my name is Louella. Jim open my legs quicker than he usually do. He ain't wait to see if I'm ready, but I didn't care, seeing his joy make me too happy to say anything. As soon as Jim try to get in Miss Lou, he loses himself.

"Dammit, God dammit," he say.

"Take your time, baby," I tell him. My man ain't big on cussing, so I know he upset.

I start rubbing his behind some more, but Jim too shamed to try again. He mumble "sorry" and get dressed and go off to the job he had for as long we been married. I pray that he don't lose that too.

After he left, I went back to sleep so I can ask Grandma Sadie what I need to do. They were waiting for me.

"Girl, I told you. You need to be more seductive," Aunt T was saying.

"Hush up, girl," my mama told her. "Can't you see she feels badly enough?"

"Look like to me she ain't feeling nothing at all," Aunt T said, laughing.

"Be quiet, y'all," Grandma Sadie told them. "Baby, listen, and listen good. I'm gonna give you the magic you need, but you got to add the spice to it. Like I said before, you've been doing the same thing the same way for years. You need to get to know every inch of that man's body and what really makes him feel good."

I tell her I thought I did. She say Jim and me don't know what we like. I figure she on the other side, so she got to know more than I do.

She say, "Baby, what I'm gonna tell you take patience and your 'bility to follow through. You got to do just what I tell you. How you do it is up to you, though."

"Tonight," she say, looking me right in the eyes, "you and Jim sit on this bed and talk about everything you think you want to do, or have done to you. It's gonna be hard, but all you can do is talk. Don't touch him no matter how hard he get. Tomorrow night you can touch each other, but you can't touch it. Then, the next night you can touch it, but don't taste. The night after, taste but don't enter. Then, on the last night, get ready to go on in."

That night, Jim came home tired as always. I cooked him his Sunday chicken dinner, and it ain't even Sunday. Jim smile at me real sweet, but say, "Baby, I don't want to try . . . let's give it some time."

I tell him, "Fine. I don't want to, but I do want to talk."

I take Jim into the bedroom, which I had cleaned real good. I had changed the bed linens and even sprinkled my best perfume on it.

"Sit down, baby. Now, Jim," I say, "for years we've been doing things the same, but we gonna try something new."

Jim start to tell me how tired he is, but I tell him to listen. He ain't really seen me act like that, but I know he like it. I sit him on the bed and undress him real slow. I never did that before either. When I take off his pants, I let my fingers touch him real light, but then I remember what my grandma say, so I stop myself. Then I undress. Now, you got to believe me when I say this . . . I don't remember the last time I got naked in front of my man with the lights on, so all this is making him crazy. I'm not as fine as I used to be, but I still look pretty good. I sit down slowly on the other side of the bed, and Jim thinks I'm asking for some.

I tell him, "Tonight, baby, we just gonna talk. Tell me what you like, and then I'll tell you. Tomorrow, you get to touch me, but you can't touch me tonight. Friday you can touch and Saturday you can touch it and taste it. Sunday, after church, if you still want to, I'll let you in."

With that, Mr. Jim came right to attention, and I was so wet I could have slid right off my bed. Just that little bit of talk done got us hot and ready, but I know that I gotta do just what Grandma Sadie say. So I start.

"Jim," I tell him, "I love the way you moan. It's telling me that it's good. I love the way you pull my knees apart, but I wish you would stroke my thighs and play with my breasts more and my nipples. I know they ain't like they used to be, but I still got feelings. I love your kisses too, but I wish . . ."

This takes me a while to say, but Jim jump up and say, "What, baby? Just tell me."

Finally, I get to it. "I wish you would kiss Miss Lou. I want you to put those big lips of yours right down there. I want you to kiss it and put your tongue on it."

I was shamed to say all that, but Jim say, "Alright, baby." He was about to do it right then, but I tell him it gotta wait.

Then, I say, "Jim, I need you to touch me more. I want you to put your hand on my head like you used to, and Jim, years ago, you used to smack me on the behind a little. I won't mind if you do that too."

Jim sure enough was grinning now. So was I. Talking about it made me want to climb on top of him and ride him to kingdom come.

"Jim," I say, "it's your turn."

Jim ain't say nothing, but I open my eyes to see his hand is holding Mr. Jim and giving himself some good love.

"Jim!" I say. "You gotta wait." I declare. I had to call him three times before he came to.

"Oh yeah. Okay. Sorry, babe. Seem like I kind of got lost."

"It's your turn," I say.

Jim say okay and tell me things that make me want to lose my mind. "Baby," he say in his deep voice, "I want you to act like you can't wait to get it."

"I can't," I almost yell.

"Well, sometimes it seems like you just doing your duty."

I don't say nothing 'cause I know I got something to learn.

"I want you to talk back too," he say. "Tell me what you want. Say it right in my ear. I want you to tell me it's good, that it's always good. I want you to put your mouth all over me."

I'm blushing now, but I try not to show it.

"Everywhere, my chest. I got nipples too, and I want your

mouth on them. Baby, I want you to put Mr. Jim in your mouth too. I want you to suck him and lick him good. I been scared to ask you for it, but we talking, ain't we?"

Jim stood up and started fondling himself again.

"We gotta wait, baby," I say.

"I know. I just want to show you how I want it. Is that okay?" Jim ask. He hold Mr. Jim up with one hand and start stroking slowly with the other. "Take your mouth up and down like this, baby," he say. "Start slow and the suck harder and faster. You can touch my balls too."

That make me want to laugh, but something tell me not to. Jim tell me to suck it 'til he say he want to come. Then he want me to stand up and bend over. He say he loves taking me from behind, but he don't do it too often because it seem like I don't like it. Now I know my grandma was right because I only remember Jim doing it twice, and both times it was so good I commence to crying. Jim must've thought I was sad, and I was too old-fashioned to tell him otherwise. I'm thinking all of this and look over to find Jim done come all over himself.

"Jim, we s'posed to wait," I say. Jim kiss me like he ain't never kiss me before and went to sleep right there in my arms.

The next day Jim wake up singing, and so do I. He called me three times from work, something he used to do back when we just got married.

"Can't wait to touch you," he say.

"Me neither," I whisper.

That night, I undress Jim again, but this time I lay him

on his stomach. I open up some of one of my grand's baby oil I found in the back of my cupboard and pour it all over his back.

"Mmm, that's nice," he say.

I rub his shoulders and back and down to his waist. I knead his strong back like I'm making bread.

"Yes, woman," he says between strokes.

Then, I pour baby oil on his behind and down between his legs. I rubbed his behind and slip my oily fingers between his cheeks. It must feel good because he snatched my hands and tried to take me right then.

"Not yet," I whisper in his ear.

"Oh, woman, you driving me crazy," he say.

"You don't know the half," I whisper back.

"Who are you, and what have you done with my wife?" he say, laughing.

"Lay down, man, and let me finish my business."

I oil his legs and rub them hard, front and back. I touch everything but Mr. Jim. Jim trying to get me to, but he know we gotta wait.

"Alright, woman," he say, "your turn."

He lay me down and pour oil right in the crack of my behind. He rubbed my behind until I thought I could see Jesus. I moaned, and Jim moaned with me. He rubbed everything but Miss Lou. I gotta tell the truth and shame the devil, Jim rubbed my feet so good, I thought I would die. I didn't know feet could get you so wet. He start at my feet and worked his way back up. When he got to my breasts, he could have asked me to run down the street buck-naked, and I might have done it! He rubbed my breasts in a way that let me know he had done it before, but not with me. I forgave him right when the thought came to me. I know that he wasn't getting this from me, and part of that is my fault. Besides, we been too far not to know how to forgive. Jim must've somehow felt my thoughts because he started to cry. I told him it was okay and held him. We rocked each other 'til we fell asleep, oily and wet.

The next day was my grocery shopping day. I got up and took a long, hot shower, fixed my hair, and put on a little makeup. Dora, who works down at the market say, "Girl, you look like you been getting some on the side." I want to tell her to hush and that she needs salvation, but I just grin. I couldn't help it, but something about what she said make me feel kinda proud. I push my pride back 'cause the Bible say pride comes before a fall and say, "Thank you." That got other folks whispering, and I let them. We live in a small town. I know folks gonna think and say whatever they want anyway.

That night, Jim came in smiling. He brought me a cup-cake from the little bakery, and it ain't even my birthday. This our night to touch Mr. Jim and Miss Lou, and neither one of us can wait. Now, I have always had my husband's dinner on the table for him when he gets home. With the exception of the birth of two of our five children and a time when I wasn't really myself, his meal has always been wait-ing. Back then, I learned a lot about real love, but I'll fill you in on that later. This time, though, I meet him on the porch. I give him some cold, tart lemonade and kiss him right on the mouth. Miss Brown from across the street is looking. I don't care, but Jim do.

"We better go in," he say.

"Let her go in if she don't like what she see."

Miss Brown must've heard me 'cause she did go in, but I saw her curtain pull back and her eye peeping through. Jim sit next to me on the porch step.

"I get to touch it tonight, don't I?" he say right up next to my ear.

His hot, sticky breath on my neck make my nipples stand out at attention, and my behind got real hot. Before I could answer, Jim shock me by slipping his hand up under my dress. Now it was already dark, so I know Miss Brown couldn't see nothing, but all of this is new to me. I was sure surprised, but I had one for Mr. Jim too. He reach under my dress and find me naked as the day I was born. I didn't have on a stitch of underwear.

"Louella Givens," he say, calling me by my maiden name.

I grin, and Jim commence to laugh like I ain't heard in years. He pull me by the hand and take me in. We didn't make it to the bedroom though. Good thing the children are grown and moved out of town, 'cause otherwise they'd seen more than they ever wanted to know. Jim lay me down right on the living room carpet and pull my dress up over my head. He start to kiss my breasts, and I remind him that he couldn't use his mouth 'til the next day. He shook his head but said he wasn't going to argue. He grab my breast with one hand and start playing with my nipple with the other. It feel too good to be true. I didn't know my nipple had that much life left in it. Then, I take one of his hands and put it down on Miss Lou.

"You full of all kinds of surprises, ain't you, woman?" Jim say.

He rub across my thighs real light for what seemed like hours. I want to scream, "Touch it, man," but I was learning the importance of patience. By the time Jim stroke the hairs on Miss Lou, I want to skip over the next few days and get right to it. Jim stroked the inside and whispered in my ear, "I love this pussy. This my pussy."

My husband had never talked like this to me before. Three days before I would have been shamed to hear this kind of talk coming from him, but that night I couldn't get enough. He stroked the inside of my kitty until it was hard as him. I was moaning and hollering like I was crazy. Then, when Jim stroked my spot, which by the way I wasn't aware of before then, I squirted all over the place like a man. I was shaking so hard, Jim came right through his pants.

"Woman," he said, "what have we been missing?"

I was panting hard and smiling like a mad woman. Jim carried me to bed. I felt too weak to touch anything he had, but it was okay. I slept until twelve midnight exactly and awoke to find Jim sleeping like a baby. I waited until one minute past and pulled Mr. Jim out of the slit of his pj's and commenced to sucking him the way Jim showed me. Jim must've done thought he was dreaming 'cause he was moaning something 'bout "No, I'm married. Please don't."

He opened his eyes and saw my mouth on him. I was

looking right in his eyes. His head rolled back, and he let out a moan that probably made Miss Brown across the street come to attention.

"I'm coming, baby." When he said that, I climbed on top of him and rocked slowly, allowing him to come inside me. Jim arched his back and yelled, "Sweet Lord, thank you."

"Yes," I said. "I'm coming with you."

We must've both passed out 'cause when I came to, Jim was lying next to me, grinning in his sleep. He woke up and smiled and started kissing me all over. He kissed as high as possible, and as low as possible, then he kissed possible. I stood up and bent over, and we did what we both like. We made love all day long. I fell asleep in between lovemaking, and I saw my ancestors.

"Girl, you was supposed to wait," Aunt T said. "You never did know how to wait."

My grandma smiled. "Girl, hush, sometimes rules are made to be broken. Besides," she added, "y'all been waiting over twenty years to get it right."

"Thank you," I told them.

Jim must've thought I was talking to him 'cause I heard him say, "You wait, you ain't had nothing to thank me for yet. Come here, woman. Let me taste you."

The Haunting of Hip Hop

A Reading Group Companion

Bertice Berry speaks to many generations in *The Haunting of Hip Hop*. Weaving together the lives of Ngozi, who was violently robbed of his ability to communicate, and Freedom, the king of chart-topping sounds, Berry raises provocative questions about the ageless importance of dialogue. We hope that the following topics will help your reading group give voice to new ideas and enjoy a spirited discussion.

1. Ngozi embodies incredible strength of character: determination, integrity, a loving heart, responsibility, respect for his family. Who are the Ngozis (male and female) in your life and community?

2. Although he named himself Freedom, Harry Hudson faces numerous obstacles, even when he is a little boy. It's only through the spirit world that he can truly set himself free. What constraints are imposed by the modern world? Can ancestors really liberate their descendants?

3. Do you share Ava's opinion of Chucky Campbell? Did he sell out?

4. The heart of the novel deals with desecration of the sacred drum: "The beat, the rhythm, the words of hip-hop music rarely spoke the truth of the drum" (Chapter 30). What is your opinion of hip-hop culture? Do raw rap lyrics contribute to violence, or do they expose a painful way of life that would otherwise go unaddressed?

5. What does the drum represent to you? How can you honor it in your own life?

6. From ragtime to jazz, doo-wop, and rap, white culture has often appropriated black musical innovations. Discuss the exploitation issues that Ava and Freedom cleverly defeat.

7. Describe the hypnotic music that Ava hears on the night of Freedom's death. If the book had come with a recording, what do you suppose this music would have sounded like?

8. From the day he is born, Ngozi's mother has many visions about his future. She tells him, "Your life here will be short, but your task is great" (Prologue), and he carries this knowledge with him into the "beast" that entombs him during the Middle Passage. In modern society, what does it take to give a child that same sense of purpose and self-worth?

9. Ngozi has no frame of reference for the kind of cruelty he sees in America, perceiving his situation as a battle of the spirits: "Once their hatred matched that of their captor, they would

have forgotten the proverb: The only weapon that can do battle with hatred is the weapon of love and peace [page 41]. . . . Ngozi was certain that the blood of the lost would be on the heads of those traitors for generations to come [page 51]." How does this philosophy relate to the daily battles in your life and to the wars being waged around the world?

10. The grandmothers represent a bridge between the novel's two main male characters, Ngozi and Freedom. How do your aunts, mothers, and grandmothers provide a link to your ancestry? How do they interact with the men in your family?

11. The brownstone sits at the corner of West 138th Street and Harriet Tubman Terrace, in a "gentrified" stretch of Harlem. What is the significance of the brownstone's location? Why do you suppose Bertice Berry included a Southern connection for so many of the characters?

12. Why did Freedom have to join the spirit world? What effect does this have on the tone of the book's final chapters?

13. The brownstone ghosts cope with a variety of unfulfilled quests. What keeps the spirits from finding peace? Which quests were you most able to identify with?

14. Are you skeptical about the existence of a spirit world, or do you feel a connection to it? Discuss any dreams, intuitive thoughts, or visions that have made a difference in your life.

15. The novel ends on a note of triumph and unity. What can be done to make this vision, Ngozi's vision, a reality?

about the author

BERTICE BERRY, Ph.D., is an
inspirational speaker, sociologist,
former stand-up comedian, and the
host of an eponymous talk show
that debuted on the Hallmark
Channel in spring 2002. She is the
author of four works of nonfiction
and the novels *Redemption Song, The
Haunting of Hip Hop,* and *Jim and
Louella's Homemade Heart-Fix Remedy.*
She lives in El Cajon, California.